When she first saw Storm, t[...]
mare, Lori knew this was th[...]
always dreamed of. When she found Storm was
for sale, she set out to earn the money and to
combat her mother's fear of horses.

But everything seemed to go wrong. Her money-
making schemes didn't turn out as she planned.
And cute, vivacious, talented Darlene entered
into a rivalry with Lori that threatened not only
her wish for Storm, but her growing relationship
with Ken as well.

POUNDING HOOVES is more than a delightful
horse story. It is the story of Lori Goodman's
struggle and triumph as she trusts God to help
her overcome her jealousy and anger, and
learns understanding and acceptance.

POUNDING HOOVES

Dorothy Grunbock Johnston

Illustrated by
Pers Crowell

David C. Cook Publishing Co.
ELGIN, ILLINOIS—WESTON, ONTARIO

POUNDING HOOVES
Copyright © 1976 David C. Cook Publishing Co.

First printing, February 1976

90 89   20 19

David C. Cook Publishing Co., Elgin, IL 60120
Printed in the United States of America
Library of Congress Catalog Number: 75-18645
ISBN: 0-912692-77-4

TO CAMI
and to all other
girls who love horses

CONTENTS

1

Pounding Hooves

THE RIGHT REAR TIRE of the school bus rolled over a rock, but the soft-leaded pencil in Lori's fingers continued deft movements. In moments, the face of a horse emerged. Flared nostrils, pricked-up ears, startled eyes, then arched tail, raised left forefoot and presto! There was the twelfth sketched horse on the page of blue-lined notebook paper.

Lori was aware that Darlene was snatching glances at what she was doing. Did Darlene think she could do better? Maybe she could. They'd both be submitting first drafts of ideas to the library committee before long.

But my drawing just has to be better than Darlene's, thought Lori. Everybody'll say,

"Some artist, and she's only fifteen. Just a sophomore." More important, I need that two-hundred-dollar prize. How else can I get enough money to replace Bucky-B?

Could Darlene read Lori's thoughts? "Too bad you have to be content with just sketches of horses," Darlene said. "Too bad you don't have a real horse on your farm anymore!"

Lori bit her lip. She tossed her head, brushed a stray black curl from her face, and turned toward the window. Darlene mustn't guess that her sarcasm had clawed way to her heart. Two

tears did manage to blur Lori's vision, but what she saw through that blur made her catch her breath.

"That horse!" Lori gasped. "Where'd she come from? She's beautiful! Chestnut with light mane and tail. What a combination! And look at that arched neck and dished-in face."

Ken Bronson's foot touched the ground lightly even before the bus lurched to a stop. He was over the gate and into the pasture in a flash, but he headed right for the house, not bothering to speak to the horse who stood alert, ready to flee.

"Look at her run!" Lori grabbed the back of the next seat. "Looks like she's scared, maybe. I wonder why? Ken never even looked in her direction."

Lori wasn't talking to Darlene, really. She didn't expect an answer. And she didn't get one. As the bus moved on, she slapped the notebook shut and rose to her feet. The Goodman mailbox loomed ahead. The next stop would be hers. Darlene got off first.

"Guess I'll grab a snack," Darlene said, "and go riding in the woods. Now that the vine-maples have turned red it's prettier than in summer down by the river. Too bad you haven't anything to ride or I might ask you to go along." The sun slanted across her long blond hair, tinting it a golden red.

11

"Couldn't go anyway," Lori mumbled. "I have other plans."

She hurried up the curved driveway that led to a weather-beaten house on a knoll, known in the community as Marycrest Farm, glad to escape from Darlene.

Lori let the door shut hard behind her. Door slamming wasn't allowed in the Goodman household. But Lori's mood was a black one at the moment. She could chew nails, almost.

"Is it you, Lori?" It was the voice of Lori's dad coming from the front room. "Come see me. Tell me how your day went."

"In a minute," Lori called. She picked up a pear and savored the sweetness. She needed time to get hold of herself. No need to let her dad see her ugly mood. Through the door she glimpsed the white cast that covered his right arm sticking out beyond the big chair where he sat watching TV. Resentment oozed up, choking her. She put the half-eaten pear down. Slowly her fingers rubbed behind the ears of the little black dog that had been bouncing and wiggling, begging for attention.

"Why did it have to happen, Posha? Tell me. Why?" Lori looked through the kitchen window, past the barn. There stood three white-faced heifers. But the dappled gray gelding was gone. Darlene had been so right. "Too bad you have to be content with just sketches of horses!" she had said.

"Content! Who's content? Not Lori Goodman! She's going to have another horse, a real live one, and soon!"

Lori let out a little sob and dropped onto the kitchen stool. Posha leaped onto her lap, nosing for her hand.

Talk was cheap and Lori knew it. How could she get a horse? Horses cost money. Winning that prize money could be only wishful thinking. She could draw. Yes. But so could Darlene and a couple dozen others in the high school. Besides, her dad said he guessed they wouldn't have any more horses on the place. Being the horse-lover he was, he could find it in his heart to shrug off the accident and go on living. But there was Lori's mother to contend with. Reared in the city, she had agreed to farm life because it was important to her husband. But she had always been afraid of horses. The accident, which had been a blow to each family member, had jelled her convictions.

"Horses cause too much grief," she stated firmly.

It would be hard to convince her otherwise. Lori's dad was inclined to go along with her, understanding her reasons. He'd been sitting around the house, slowed down by that shattered elbow for a month already and it would be a while, yet, before he could get back to running a press at the *Herald*. Bills were piling up. Doctor bills. Grocery bills.

"What we don't need is a big hay bill on top of it all," he conceded when his wife pointed it out. Reluctantly, he agreed to Bucky-B's being taken to the auction the Saturday after that fateful day.

When Mom was out of earshot he tried to console Lori by saying, "Maybe, someday, when the mountain of bills is paid—we didn't have much insurance, you know, and medical bills shot up to nearly three thousand dollars overnight, almost. Wiped out all our savings. Maybe, someday we can get another horse. We'll be sure to find one that's already well trained. But right now I don't want to cause your mother any more worry."

"Maybe! Someday!" It was all too far away and too indefinite to suit Lori.

"If only Dad hadn't reached up and moved his hat to scratch his head!" Lori complained into Posha's ear. "Bucky-B was only green broke. He didn't know about hats. He should have been allowed to sniff it. It should have been waved in front of him. A man on his back was kind of a new experience. And a man wearing a hat—well, he just spooked, that's all. The

14

lunge forward caught Dad off guard. If only he'd had hold of those reins!"

Lori shuddered. She knew that being dragged by a horse with one foot in a stirrup could have banged her dad up a lot worse.

Actually, they were all thankful it was only a shattered elbow. That word "shattered" was revealing. It told why the whole ordeal was so expensive. Specialists had to be called in. There were two, no, three operations. Thankful it was *only* a shattered elbow? Well, yes. But that one elbow had changed her whole world!

"You coming, Lori?" Her dad's voice brought Lori back to the here and now.

"Yes, I'm coming," she called, trying to sound cheerful. "Want a pear?" Lori moved toward the front room. "Here." She bent down and pecked him on the forehead and he playfully tugged at her long hair with his left hand.

"How'd things go today?" he asked. "Get any ideas for that mural design?" He glanced at the calendar. "Just four more weeks . . . twenty-seven days to be exact — to get your plan in. You're going to win, I feel sure. You'll get a horse or two in the picture and nobody can draw horses like you can!"

Lori laughed. "Don't be so sure," she said. "Darlene is pretty good. She says she knows she is the one who'll be painting that mural in the library. Something's got to give. We can't both do it!"

Lori left the room and returned with her notebook, flipping the pages. "Which sketch do you like best?" she asked. "If I plan my design around the horse pose I do best, I'll have a better chance, don't you think?"

She watched her dad's face as he studied the sketches. His intense expression reminded her that the love of his life, next to his family, was horses. Five years before, it was Lori's dad who had surprised her with a pony on her tenth birthday. Brushing, bridling, saddling, she'd learned from him. More than that, he had taught her the importance of cultivating a camaraderie between horse and rider so that they moved and thought as one.

Lori knew how much her father liked the soft nicker of a horse who was his friend. Often she'd seen him leaning on a fence rail, entranced, watching the grace and symmetry of a galloping horse. Bucky-B had cavorted around the field in the evening in sheer exuberance, it seemed. At the sound of pounding hooves, her dad had always dropped what he was doing just so he could watch—and listen to the rhythm of the galloping.

No more horses on the place? You're wrong, Dad. You don't know it, but there's going to be a horse here, one you'll ride and enjoy riding. You just wait and see!

"This is your best bet." Lori's dad's left forefinger pointed to the sketch she had done on the bus. "It's got life and movement. Look at that mane and tail! And the raised foreleg. No judge could pass up a horse like that. Reminds me of Bucky-B." His voice trailed off.

Lori knew he was remembering and regretting Mom's urgent insistence that horses were no longer to be a big part of his life. Lori was glad he didn't know what she was thinking: *You just wait and see, Dad. You're in for a surprise. A big surprise!*

Mr. Goodman put the notebook aside. "Your mother left a message for you," he said. "She made chili before she went to work. But she wants you to put a dessert into the oven. I picked up a bucket of windfalls. How about an apple pie?"

"Mind if I change that to apple cake, Dad? It's quicker. There's something I have to do. I have to see, well, that is, I noticed blackberries along the road by the Silver Spurs Ranch. When the timer goes off, take the cake out, will you please? Think you can manage it? Where's Mike? He can help."

No need to mention that the tangle of blackberry vines lined the fence of Bronsons' pasture and that the berries were only an excuse to get another look at that beautiful horse. Could she be an Arabian? She must be part-Arabian, at least, Lori guessed. Dad's feelings about horses were mixed at the moment. He didn't really blame Bucky-B. If only he'd kept control. . . .

But you can't build the future on "if only. . . ."

Lori brushed her thoughts away and found the recipe, then began to peel apples. She was sifting flour when a rumble on the stairs told her that Mike was emerging from his room, looking for excitement.

"Say 'Hi' to Mr. Midget!" Mike demanded.

He rubbed his chin against the soft fur of the small rodent peeking from inside his shirt collar.

"Oh, take that rat out of the kitchen!" demanded Lori. "It gives me the creeps!"

"It's not a rat, it's a gerbil and you know it!" Mike shot back. He lowered his voice. "Well, it is a desert rat, really. But so what? He's my pet and he's cute. Say 'Hi' to Mr. Midget!"

This time Mike held the tiny animal in cupped hands right under Lori's nose. The gerbil stared at her with beady black eyes and twitched his whiskers.

"Hi, Mr. Midget!" growled Lori. "Now take that varmint away. Can't you see I'm trying to get a cake into the oven? You know how short the days are now. I'm leaving. Going berry-picking."

"Don't mind her," Mike told his pet, stroking its fur with a forefinger. "The only animal that excites Sis, here, is a horse." Then, remembering, he turned to his sister. "Did you notice what's running around in Bronsons' pasture?" His hazel eyes widened and his freckled pug nose wiggled. "I was walking by and an apple fell. Off she went. Talk about a spooky horse! Wonder where Bronsons got her. Is it Ken's horse or his dad's?"

"How do I know?" Lori snapped. Ten-year-old brothers could be a nuisance, asking silly questions. She wondered herself. That's why she ached to get that cake into the oven, grab a pail and be off.

Mike drifted into the front room. He and his dad were watching Mr. Midget munch a sunflower seed when Lori called, "I'm leaving, now, Dad. Be sure to take that cake out when the bell rings." She waited to make sure her dad heard.

"OK," he called.

"I'm going on my bike and I'll be back in time to set the table. No, have Mike do it. I'll pick a cucumber for the salad from the patch on my way back. We can be ready to sit down when Mom gets here."

Lori swung the pail as she skipped toward the shed on the north side of the barn. Then, remembering, she slowed to a walk. There was no bridle

19

over her arm. Those happy days of going for a horseback ride every day after school had been so short-lived. Bucky-B always behaved for her. Of course, she had taken it slow and easy, talking to him in a low friendly voice and making sure always to have an apple or carrot in her pocket, or maybe a handful of oats. She'd learned that trick when getting acquainted with Patches, her pony, whom she had outgrown and traded in as part-payment for Bucky-B. Now spiders busily spun webs in Bucky's stall.

Pushing the shed door open, Lori slipped inside. Hands on hips, she stared at the battered blue bike. What good was a bike? You couldn't talk to it or pet it or feed it or win it for a friend. It could get you somewhere faster than you could walk. That was about all.

"Take me to the Silver Spurs Ranch—fast, you old iron horse," Lori said.

She slipped the pail onto the handlebars and headed down the drive. She'd pick berries and keep her eyes open. She was curious about that horse.

And maybe, just maybe, she'd see Ken.

2

The Arabian

A STICK IN HER LEFT HAND to push back the prickly vines, Lori used her deft right fingers to seek out plump juicy blackberries. The plinkity-plunk sound of berries dropping into the pail had ceased as the berries piled up. The softest and ripest she popped into her mouth.

She kept glancing from one end of the pasture to the other, longing for another look at that beautiful horse. To Lori's disappointment, she was nowhere in sight. There wasn't even any sign of Ken around the low-slung ranch house nestled among the fruit trees. Her curiosity about the mare would have been a casual way to get to talk to Ken. She sighed and sought out a new spot to pick berries, ones that weren't dried and shriveled by the early October sun.

Across the road, almost hidden by vines and brush were the tumbledown remains of a house, once the home of early pioneers. Lori had often explored it, trying to reconstruct the simple life of the family that had lived there. There was an outhouse, a woodshed, an old well. Pages from magazines had been used as wallpaper to keep out the cold. She loved to read those yellowed pages, especially the ads for liniment and for Lydia E. Pinkham pills which they claimed every woman needed to be in sparkling good health.

But there was no time to prowl around in the old house today.

Lori's thoughts drifted to the mural design. She needed to go to the old Jeffrey place to sketch the log cabin with its moss-covered roof, and the hand pump outside the kitchen door. She had to decide where to add the figure of the horse her dad had chosen to give life to the pioneer scene. Maybe a barefooted kid pumping water into the pail would be good. Yes, that's what it needed. Water actually pouring from the pump would make the whole thing come to life.

Much as she hated to admit it, the close-cropped curls and freckled face of Mike would make him a perfect model. She wondered if she could get him to pose for her. Probably have to bribe him. When he knew she needed him he could get real bratty.

Lori could see the completed picture in her mind's eye. She'd make it an autumn scene so she could use yellow maple trees and the brilliant red vine-maple leaves to contrast with the deep green of evergreens in the background.

Lori was startled to hear the crunch of feet on the gravel road leading from the ranch house. Was Ken coming and she hadn't seen him? She peered around the mountain of berry vines.

"Oh, hello, Mr. Bronson," she called.

"Hi, Lori." Ken's dad took the evening paper from the can.

"I'm getting berries for a pie. Maybe jam, too."

"Picking berries, are you? Why don't you come on in? Berries get dusty here by the road. There's a great clump in the south end of the pasture. I noticed that Storm's been nibbling at them. But she can't get many. An Arab's skin is so sensitive, she stays clear of the prickles." He held the gate open, waiting. Lori slipped through, murmuring her thanks as she went, and he pulled the gate shut behind her.

"Storm?" queried Lori. "Is that the name of the mare I saw from the school bus? Where is she? She's a dream of a horse!"

"Glad you think so," Mr. Bronson said. "Ken

despises her, if you can believe it. Says Arabs are too sensitive. Have to be handled carefully and gently. And he's the one I bought her for, too. It's sure a disappointment to me."

"Where'd you find her?"

"I saw her when I was down in Sultan and found I could have her — for a price. I loaded her right up and brought her home with me. That was where I made my mistake. Since I was buying the horse for Ken, I should have consulted him. Made sure I was buying a horse he liked. His idea of a good horse and mine aren't the same, it seems." The sag of Mr. Bronson's shoulders and the slowness of his feet told Lori that a dream had collapsed.

The two were nearing the weather-beaten barn. Lori was about to say good-bye and head for the berries in the south pasture when Mr. Bronson said, "Want another look at Storm? She's in a stall, here. Ken's cleaning out the barn. We won't be in his way. Come on in."

Suddenly the clatter of hooves against the barn wall rumbled like thunder. Hurriedly, Mr. Bronson pushed back the catch and swung the barn door open.

"What's all the commotion?" he demanded. "What's going on in here?"

Lori stood on tiptoe to see over his shoulder. A gaping hole in the rear of the stall and splintered wood scattered everywhere held her attention for only a moment. Frantically, Ken was reaching for the mare's lead rope, while her rear hooves were striking at the wall.

"Settle down, you fool horse!" he shouted.

Lori pushed past Ken's dad. She flung the pail of berries into a manger. Her right hand shot out to grab the lead rope which Ken had not yet been able to grasp.

"Step back!" ordered Lori.

Ken moved back, glad to be relieved of the responsibility of quieting the horse. On the third try, Lori closed her hand over the rope snapped to the horse's halter. Quickly, Lori tied the loose end of the short rope to the manger.

"Pulled the rope loose, did you? Well, settle down!" Lori yanked the rope hard a few times. The mare pulled back, reaching her head high, her eyes rolling. But she stopped kicking.

Lori had pocketed an apple on her way to the barn. She now offered it to the mare, speaking in low, soft tones. "Quiet, old girl. It's not that bad. What upset you? You have hay. And here's an apple. A nice juicy apple. We aren't going to hurt you."

The horse sniffed at the apple, then moved her head away with a jerk. Three times she sniffed at the apple on the up-turned palm. But she did not touch it.

Ken picked up the pitchfork he had thrust aside when the horse began to kick.

"All I did was push a wheelbarrow behind her and she let her hind feet fly. No wonder those boys named her 'Storm.' Should have called her 'Hurricane' or 'Tempest.' Some horse! And I'm supposed to get excited over her. No, thanks!"

Lori held tight to the lead rope, and made unsuccessful attempts to pat the mare's head. She listened for Ken's dad's answer. He said nothing, only looked dismayed.

Ken went on. "Now we've got this huge hole in the barn to patch. That's all I needed. One more job. On a beautiful day like this when the humpies are spawning in the river." Ken turned to his father. "Why don't you turn her out, Dad? I can't clean the barn with her in here!"

Mr. Bronson sighed. "You know why she's in here. If we let her loose again, we'll never be able to catch her. It took three of us to corner her and head her inside as it was."

"Yeah," Ken admitted. "Mom wasn't any too happy about having to come out to help, either."

"You'll have to wheel the manure out the back door. Try not to startle her with any loud noises. She has to be handled carefully until she learns that we're her friends. Those boys sure did a first-rate job of spooking her!"

"No wonder the manager was so willing to be rid of her when you asked if she was for sale!"

"But as she stood there in the pasture I thought she had the best conformation of any horse I'd seen for a good long time."

Mr. Bronson took a large red handkerchief from his right rear pocket and mopped his brow.

"It sure was a mistake, bringing this mare on the place. Now, what's the next thing to do? I won't even be able to sell her."

Ken agreed. "No one wants to buy a horse you can't catch or get near to with a saddle, even on a ten-foot pole."

"I didn't know all the tricks those boys had played on her until after I got her. What a mess!"

While listening to the son and the father voice their feelings, Lori again held the apple for the mare to accept if she would. Finally, Lori's curiosity exploded.

"What boys?" she demanded. "Who's been abusing a horse like this? Where'd you get her, anyway?"

Ken went back to cleaning the stall next to Storm, one used by his dad's heifers, trying not to make any unexpected noises. Lori continued to hold onto the lead rope with her right hand, just in case Storm was startled again. Mr. Bronson sat down on a bale of hay and crossed his legs.

"I was delivering a couple of goats to the boys' school up the River Road, the place where they take in boys who need help one way or another. Some old man had owned the mare, here, and he'd given her to the boys. Trouble was, she'd never been broken and she was already four years old. That's pretty late to start training. To top it all, the boys knew nothing about horses. City kids, mostly. But they figured if you had a horse, there must be some way to ride her."

"They spooked her for sure," Lori said. "How'd they do it?"

"They got hold of a saddle somehow and, with ropes, hung it from the barn rafters. They got the horse below and tried to lower the saddle onto her back. With this great unknown thing coming at her from above, of course she spooked."

28

Lori nodded. "That's why she's extra nervous here in this barn right now."

Ken's dad went on. "I didn't know all this until after I'd brought her home. I called back and got the lowdown. 'Course I knew we had a hard time loading her onto the truck. But then, a lot of otherwise good horses get excited when being loaded. So I didn't think too much about that." He wiped his brow again. "What a mistake!"

Lori had tied the lead rope securely, but the horse kept moving her hindquarters from side to side, ready to let those hind feet fly should that wheelbarrow rumble past her rear again. She kept her ears pricked back, alert for the signal to kick.

"Let me gentle her, Mr. Bronson. Please do. I can stop over every afternoon after school. I'll take it slow and easy." She studied Mr. Bronson's face to see if she could tell his reaction. "Bucky-B was pretty wild when we got him, but I was getting along just fine with him. It wasn't really his fault. . . ." Lori stopped short. She always felt guilty, saying it was her dad's negligence that had caused the horse to throw him. It was true. But she'd leave it unsaid this time.

Mr. Bronson's blue eyes lip up. "Why, sure!" he said. "I believe you've got something there. It takes a teenage girl fussing over a horse day

29

after day. Best way to gentle a horse I know of. And you're an experienced horsewoman. I remember the way you handled that pony you got when you were just a kid. It didn't try any funny stuff on you! Once, maybe, but not twice!"

Lori laughed. "I was awfully handy at yanking an alder branch from a tree and stripping the leaves off. Just the sight of that fast-made whip in my hand made Patches settle down. Seldom had to really use the whip. Just had to show it to him, usually."

"Sure. Come on over. Come every day. Help yourself to windfalls, like you did just now, to make your job easier. There's always oats here in the barn. Storm's no good to anyone the way she is. Gentle her and maybe I can get my money back out of her. How much you going to charge me for gentling this horse? Tell me that!"

Lori laughed happily. "Charge you, Mr. Bronson? Are you kidding?" She turned to the mare. "You're not all that bad, are you, Storm?"

Lori tried to brush her cheek against the horse's cheek. But Storm raised her head high, shying away.

"Mr. Bronson, did you say you want to sell her? May I have first choice? I don't know how I'd ever pay for her. How much would she be?"

Mr. Bronson stood up, feeling in a manger beneath the hay.

"Just as I thought," he said. "That banty has been trying to steal a nest again." He filled both hands with eggs, then looked around the edge of the haymow for an oats can to put them into. "Well," he said. "I'd have to get three and a quarter for her. That's what I paid for her. And I'd be out all the feed from the time I got her until I get rid of her. Why don't you take her right now, Lori?"

"Oh, I couldn't do that!" There was alarm in Lori's brown eyes. "I couldn't upset my dad. It's only been a month, you know, since . . . well, since the accident. He's not too anxious to have another horse on the place. I guess you can understand why. If I brought home a wild horse, one you can't catch or ride, well . . . it just wouldn't work. Let's wait until she's gentle and well behaved. Besides, I don't have the money just now. How much did you say? You mentioned three and a quarter. You mean three hundred dollars . . . and twenty-five more?"

Mr. Bronson nodded. "That's right. It's three hundred and twenty-five dollars. Wish I could just give her to you, Lori. But you know how it is. If Ken ever decides on a horse, I'll need the money from this one to swing the deal."

Ken was slipping out of his rubber boots, his job over.

"Tell it like it is, Dad," he said. "You weren't

31

planning to give me a horse. I was earning one. But while I'm taking care of your white-faced cattle, I might as well be earning myself a horse I like."

The three left the barn and were walking toward the apple trees that surrounded the house. Ken reached up and plucked an orange and yellow-striped Gravenstein, then two more, tossing one to Lori, one to his dad.

"Want something to munch?" he asked, as he bit into the apple.

"Thanks," Lori said, catching the apple. She flashed a smile at Ken. Were anybody's eyes bluer than his? she wondered. He often wore a blue shirt, like now, making his eyes seem more blue.

Too bad his brown hair is so straight, Lori thought. Then she felt like kicking herself. Ken with waves? He wouldn't be Ken!

Ken pointed. "Now, there's a horse—a man's horse! Get rid of this Storm and get me Rowdy, Dad." Ken raised his voice. "Hi, Joe," he called.

Charging up from the far gate came a boy on a brown and white gelding. The horse snorted and pawed, wheeled, then tossed his head. The pale blue behind his brown eyes gave him a wild, unmanageable look.

"Steady there, Rowdy, old boy," Joe said, pulling on the reins.

"We were just talking about horses," Ken told Joe. "I'm not a guy who just has to have a horse. They're OK. But I'm not wild about them. The only reason I'd want a horse would be so I could get down to the river quicker after my chores are done."

"The humpies are in. Right?" Joe interrupted.

"Right!" Ken said. "I could tie my wetsuit to a horse and be down to the river in no time, almost. That is, if I had a horse I could *trust*." The look Ken gave first to Lori, then his father, had significance. "Then I'd tie the horse to a tree, pull on my wetsuit and swim around at the bottom of the river with the salmon. That way I could observe how they swim, the changes in their snouts as the spawning season progresses, and I could maybe make a good report to the Department of Fisheries. Can you see me doing all that with that old nag, Storm? She'd shy at being tied to a tree. Probably get skittish over a bee buzzing. Then she'd get herself a ropeburn and be lame for the rest of the spawning season. No, thanks. Give me a horse like Rowdy, here."

Joe grinned. "Up, boy. Up!" he said. Rowdy reared up on his hind legs, pawing the air with his front feet, then eased back to a standing position. "Up!" commanded Joe. As his horse's front feet touched the ground again, Joe's knees pressed into the horse's side and away Rowdy dashed. Joe let out a cry, imitating a Comanche Indian. He rode his mount in a circle a couple of times, then brought him up to an abrupt halt before his three spectators.

"Hey," Ken said. "That's a man's horse. If you ever want to sell Rowdy, let me be the first to know, Joe."

"You've got to be kidding!" Joe grinned. "Rowdy's not for sale, are you, old boy?" Joe leaned forward, patting Rowdy affectionately on the neck. He turned to Ken. "What are you doing? Want to go to the river? I don't suppose you can ride that new horse of yours. I hear she's got a mind of her own."

"I guess I'm free for an hour," Ken said, glancing at his father to get the OK signal. "Sure, I want to go to the river. That barn can wait until tomorrow to be patched. But I don't want to be reduced to a bike like Lori."

"Stupid!" Joe said. "Rowdy can carry us both. Hop on. We'll ride double."

Ken climbed the rail fence, took a run and sprinted up onto Rowdy's back from over his rump.

"Couldn't do that to a temperamental fussy old Arabian," Ken called over his shoulder as Rowdy danced forward.

In an instant they were by the far gate. Joe leaned down and swung the gate open wide enough for Rowdy to pass through, then Ken pulled it shut behind, neither having to dismount.

Both boys waved, both boys let out yells and they were off. Lori stood on the lowest rail of the fence, then climbed to the second rail to see the boys better above the tangle of blackberry vines.

"Good-bye, Ken," she called. And as an afterthought, she added, "Good-bye, Joe."

Soon they were out of sight. Only the sound of pounding hooves told them that Ken was headed to do what he loved most.

Ken had been only eight the first time he saw an adult salmon struggling up the small stream in the ravine on the backside of their ranch. His dad hadn't been able to answer all his questions. Finally, to make peace, Ken's mother had come back from the library loaded with books about the migrations and spawning habits of salmon. She'd even sent to the State Department of Fisheries for literature. The fine print intended for college students hadn't dismayed the young scientist. He'd devoured and digested the facts and every time he had a choice of subjects to write about or talk about at school, it was salmon.

"That's some kid!" Mr. Bronson said, turning back toward the barn, a wide grin on his face.

Lori could tell he was proud of his son. He

wasn't too upset, really, over Ken's disdain for the horse he had picked for him. It would all work out, somehow.

Now Lori remembered her pail. "I set my pail down in a manger when all the excitement started," she said. "I'll get it and pick berries in the south pasture." She paused at the door of the barn. "I'll be back tomorrow, if it's settled that I'm to try to gentle Storm. I'll do my best, Mr. Bronson."

Lori was about to leave when she noticed a flashy red car drive into the area between the road and the gate.

"You expecting company, Mr. Bronson? Somebody's here."

3

A Bright Idea

LORI DIDN'T STAY in the south pasture long. She became alarmed when the sky began to glow. Pink, almost crimson clouds hovered over the mountains in the west. She was due home long before sunset. There was the salad to make and the last minute things to get ready before her mother came home, tired.

It would be quicker to strike out for home through the woods beyond the pasture by foot. But she'd left her bike near Bronsons' barn and she'd better go back after it.

The stranger was still talking to Mr. Bronson in persuasive tones.

"I'm not making a deal. That's final!" Ken's dad said as Lori came around the corner of the barn. Looking up, he noticed her. "You back, Lori? Meet Mr. Katz, here. Carl Katz. He's bound and determined he's going to buy my barn. I've decided he's not!"

Lori and Mr. Katz said "Hi" to each other. Lori slipped her berry pail onto the handlebars. She mounted the bike and sat poised ready to take off.

"You mean you want just the barn? Not the whole ranch, house and land and all?"

Mr. Katz grinned. "You're right, young lady. The barn is all I'm interested in. You see, there's a new rage. Folks building fancy houses or restaurants want weather-beaten boards to add interest to one interior wall. Recreation rooms are a favorite. Mr. Bronson could make himself a pile if he'd agree to sell."

Ken's dad looked up at the pair of elk antlers near the peak of the barn.

"This place has historic value," he said. "The old bachelor who cleared the place and built the cabin beyond our ranch house split the cedar shakes for this barn by hand. The huge stump out there in the field is where he cut one of the trees with a crosscut saw."

"It's picturesque, I'll admit," nodded Mr. Katz. "But you conceded that the roof leaks. Moldy hay can make animals sick, I'm sure you know. Now, wouldn't a nice new barn look good

38

to you? What I'd pay for your hand-split weather-beaten cedar shakes would pay for the finest modern barn in the county and you'd have money in your pocket, besides!"

Mr. Bronson shook his head.

"Here's my card. Hang onto it in case you change your mind." The real estate salesman headed toward his red car beyond the last gate.

Ken's dad was poking the business card into a crack by the high window of the first stall as Lori called a good-bye and started home.

It was almost too dark to see any cucumbers as Lori passed the garden on her way to the house. The underside of the vines prickled her hand as she felt for the smooth-sided vegetables. She found three and hurried inside, berry pail in hand.

Chili steamed on the stove. A hurried glance at the table in the other end of the kitchen told Lori that Mike had minded for once, and had set the table.

"Hi, Mom!" Lori forced a smile, not sure yet if she was in trouble for being so late. "Sorry I'm late. But I got berries. Is jam hard to make? I'd like to try. How'd your day go?"

Lori's mother peered into the berry pail. "You did get a bucketful of berries," she said. "It would have been nice, though, if supper had been ready when I walked in." She glanced out the window. "The days are getting shorter and I suppose you didn't notice. Well, let's make the salad so we can sit down."

Lori sighed, relieved. Mom wasn't too mad. In fact, she had as good as forgiven her. Now to get dinner over so she could work on her sketch for the mural. Her dad was only too right. It was due in 27 days and time would have wings.

At the table, Lori described Storm in glowing word-pictures—the velvet-smooth chestnut skin, a smoothness that only a well-bred horse has, the startling beauty of the light mane and tail, flaxen against her dark hide.

"When I first saw her from the bus window, I knew I'd never seen such a dream of a horse!" exclaimed Lori, her brown eyes wide, remembering. "That long sleek neck, arched slightly from the base of the ears to the withers . . . the way she holds her tail when she runs. And the contrast of the light mane and tail with the rest of her. Oh, I tell you, she's a beauty!"

"Please pass the bread," was all Lori's dad said.

Lori glanced at him, wondering. Was he interested in hearing about the new horse over at Silver Spurs? Or did the mention of horses upset him? Wearing that heavy cast was getting old, Lori knew.

Somehow, Lori sensed that her dad was interested, although he didn't want to appear that way. So between bites of beans, Lori bubbled on.

"I wanted berries, yes. But really, I have to admit, it was a good excuse to get a better look at that mare. . . ."

"Bet you didn't get close to her!" Mike blurted out. "Randy told me nobody can get near her."

Lori sent Mike a withering look. "You're so wrong, Mr. Know-it-all! I was in the barn right beside her stall and I had hold of her!"

No need to tell why it had been necessary for her to grab the mare's lead rope, no need to mention the hole in the barn caused by her flailing hooves.

Lori turned to her father. "I wish you could see her profile up close, Dad. Her face is dished just right. It's hard to describe her muzzle, but somehow it looks the way a horse ought to look. And her eyes are well apart. That means she's intelligent, doesn't it, Dad?" If only she could get some response from her father!

Mr. Goodman buttered another piece of homemade bread and spooned strawberry jam onto it before he answered. It gave Lori time to get at her food. Cabbage, green grape, cantaloupe and cucumber salad was a favorite, but she'd been talking so much she hadn't had time to eat.

41

Finally her dad said, "Yes, it's generally considered to be a sign of intelligence, a good distance between the eyes. But what were this mare's ears like? You can get an idea of a horse's disposition by the way she holds her ears. If they were pointed back a good bit of the time, it mean's she's nervous and has a bad disposition. Bucky-B carried his ears in an alert, interested manner. He wasn't mean. Just green broke, was all."

Lori gulped. She hadn't meant to mention that Storm's ears were mostly pointed back.

"Her ears? Funny thing, I hardly noticed them. But she has well-shaped hooves. That's an important part of a horse. You can't ride them if they don't have good feet!"

"Why all the enthusiasm?" asked Lori's mother. "Mr. Bronson probably bought this mare for Ken. You sound as though he bought her for you!"

"Yes, but Ken . . . well." Lori's face turned tomato red. "It's just that I need a model, a horse to look at when I design the mural. I'm glad I have such a super horse to look at. Don't you think that's nice?"

"Very nice, dear."

Lori looked out of the corner of her eye at her mother. Had she said too much too enthusiastically? Did her mother guess that she maybe had some sort of plot? Better change the subject fast.

But before she thought of anything to say, her dad was speaking.

"You miss Bucky-B, don't you, Lori?"

Oh, oh! What else is Dad going to say?

"Ken is probably pretty proud, owning such a fine horse," Lori's dad went on. No doubt he'll be going down to the river often. But when she's in the pasture, you can pet her. Ken wouldn't care, I'm sure. It's nice to have a horse for a friend. But I don't want you riding her. Mine wasn't the first or only horse accident. They happen oftener than you think." He glanced at his wife. "Our family has written horses off as a bad dream."

He doesn't believe that! Lori told herself. That little speech was for Mom's benefit. She's the one who doesn't want any of us to get onto a horse again. Dad might hesitate, because of that elbow. But he has guts. Once over the first tense moment, he'd love riding just as he always has!

Mr. Goodman looked at Lori again. "By the way, you haven't told us the mare's name. Isn't she called something besides 'the mare'?"

"You bet she is!" Mike's voice somehow sounded shrill. "That mare's name is Storm! I don't know why, but I bet there's a good reason. Probably kicks up a storm if you try to get near her."

Lori thought, if only I'd changed the subject sooner! She kicked Mike under the table and coughed a little.

She jumped up. "Who wants some apple cake?"

She hurried across the kitchen and made a clatter getting down the dessert plates. As far as Lori was concerned, there'd be no more talk about the Bronson horse that night.

The dishes done, Lori did her math homework, then joined the others who were watching TV. She could watch, or at least listen, and sketch at the same time. After a few minutes, she threw the pad down in disgust.

"I'm not getting anywhere. I have to go back to the old Jeffrey place. I can't remember what the pump looks like. I need to see the water gush out. I need to see just how the person pumping holds the handle. Hey, Mike, how about being my model? We can go over right after school tomorrow."

"Me? What are you going to give me for going?"

"Give you? All you have to do is pump a little water from an old well. Is that going to be so hard to do? Honestly! You can be so pesty! And when I really need you and want to be

44

friends, you need to be bribed! If it's money you want, I don't have any! I'll ask Randy. He's a good kid, even if he is Darlene's brother. He won't want any pay!"

Randy wouldn't want to be in his sister's competitor's picture, either, Lori suddenly realized. "I'll tell you what, Mike. I'll draw a great huge picture of you for your bedroom wall. You'll have your own custom-made poster!"

"It's a deal if you'll put Mr. Midget in, too. Let's do it now."

Mike ran to his room for his pet.

When Mike came back with the tiny animal peeking from a shirt sleeve, Lori was on hands and knees on the kitchen floor, a huge sheet of paper before her, sketching pencil in hand.

"Sit any way you want," she said. "Where do you want Mr. Midget?"

Mike sat cross-legged on the floor, holding the gerbil on an open palm, watching his pet nibble paper.

"You'd think Mr. Midget would get tired of chewing paper, wouldn't you? Look at those little jaws go up and down. And look at the hole in the paper! You're the chewingest gerbil, Mr. Midget." Mike turned to his sister. "You through, Lori?"

"I can sketch just so fast," Lori said. "Now sit still, will you?"

Actually, he's a cute subject, Lori was thinking. The curly hair, pug nose and freckles will go just right with ragged blue jeans, bare feet and an old-fashioned pump. But why does he have to be so bratty, sometimes? Like blurting out Storm's name as though it really fit. It does, of course, but I was going to leave that part out.

"There! You can put Mr. Midget away if you want. Or just let him go up your sleeve if you can get him to stop chewing paper," Lori told her brother. "I'm through with him."

The finished product wasn't a real portrait. It was more of a caricature. The hair was extra curly, the nose a little too pug, and the freckles too thick. Mr. Midget's jaws bulged with paper. But anyone could tell at a glance that it was Mike and Mr. Midget. Mike was delighted, and after showing the poster-sized sketch to his folks, he rummaged in the kitchen drawer for tape, then bounded off to his room to put the poster on his wall.

Well, that was settled. Mike would go along willingly as a model. Lori might have to put off going with him until Saturday. She'd have to stop by to see Storm after school tomorrow and the day after. That was a must. There might not be time before supper to do both, especially when Mom would probably leave instructions for supper preparations.

Then there was that jam to make. This having her mother working all day and depending on Lori to do what she used to do was a drag. She had always helped around the house, both inside and out. Her Dad liked to read the Bible and quote it. One of his favorite sayings was, "If you don't work, you can't eat." That's not the exact way the Bible put it. But that's what it meant. There was something else about watching the ants and copying them. It all added up to the fact that everyone in the Goodman household had jobs to do and did them. Lori had no quarrel with that. It was just that she hated the newly placed responsibility. When dinner being served on time depended on her, it cramped her style.

Oh, well, Lori thought. Dad's tired of staying home, Mom's tired of not staying home, and we all have to adjust—all but Mike. His life hasn't changed much. He has more time with his father, if anything. But at least, I have Storm. Not only do I *get* to see her every day, I *have* to. Mr. Bronson is depending on me. What a horse! What a challenge!

But as Lori mounted the stairs to her room, her feet dragged. She remembered that as soon as Storm was gentle, and could be ridden and trusted, if that was possible, then Ken's dad would sell her.

What if Ken changed? What if he liked Storm after all, when someone else had had the patience to win her friendship, convincing her that the human race wasn't her enemy? Then Storm wouldn't be for sale! Ken'd probably let Lori ride her. But she needed a horse of her own, one she could share with her dad. His life wouldn't be complete until he had the courage and opportunity to ride again. Maybe Mom didn't understand that, but Lori did.

But if Ken still held out for what he called "a man's horse, not a fool Arabian," and Storm had to be sold to get Ken a horse he liked, what then?

Over three hundred dollars! What teenager has money like that? Not me!

In her room, Lori opened the top dresser drawer and pulled out her bankbook.

Just thirty-seven measly dollars. If I'd only known I could have picked strawberries faster last June. Or I could have baby-sat during the summer. Can't do either, now. No strawberries in the fall. And my time's not my own, now. If they keep Storm or sell Storm, either way, I'm licked!

Lori sank to the bed, dejected. Automatically, her hands reached for her hair. After brushing it, she divided it and began to braid.

Anyway, Storm will be mine, all mine, for one hour tomorrow. Wonder how I'll get along?

Mixed up in Lori's dreams that night were visions of a mare jerking her head, her ears pointed back against her head, gleaming teeth showing in a wide, mocking grin. Next, Lori was calling, but the mare was galloping, not toward her, but further and further away. In her outstretched hand, Lori held an apple. On she stumbled. But the light mane and tail on that beautiful chestnut horse were just a speck in the distance.

And in her ears echoed the sickening sound of pounding hooves!

4

Storm's Handshaking Lesson

AFTER SCHOOL THE NEXT DAY, Lori felt obligated
to make an apple pie. She couldn't ignore her
dad's gentle insistence that that was why he
had picked up windfalls with his good left hand.
Lori had come to realize that little things were
important to a person who is sick or disabled. If
her dad wanted apple pie so badly she'd better
make him one. At least she didn't have to make
the entire dinner. There was jello salad in the
refrigerator and her mother had a casserole ready
to put into the oven. It and the pie could bake
at the same time. That way she could head for
Silver Spurs Ranch for that one delicious hour
she had waited for all day. Her fingers flew. At
last, the pie was crimped and in the oven. Dad

would take out the casserole and pie when they were done.

Lori's iron horse got her over the Old Burn Road in minutes. Would Storm still be in her stall or would she be out in the pasture?

There she was! Watching Lori unlatch the gate, swing it open, slip her bike through the opening, shut the gate and lock it again. Ears pointed forward, alert, then rotating back in alarm. Snorting, sniffing, pawing. The horse, so beautiful to look at, was all nervousness and anxiety.

Would she and this mistreated animal ever develop a friendship? Lori hardly dared to hope that they would. But she would try.

Suddenly, the horse bolted to the far side of the pasture. The rumble of her hooves was drowned out by the approaching tractor.

"Hi, Lori," called Mr. Bronson, bringing the tractor to a stop. "Sorry I had to let the mare out. Couldn't go on feeding her hay when there's still grass in the field. If you want to—and can—you can put her in the barn for your training session. But turn her loose before you go home." He started to move off. "Good luck!" he called.

Lori nodded to show she understood the message. It was hard to talk over the noise of the tractor. The farmer would unload the sled of wood he was pulling toward the woodshed near the house, then head back into the woods for another load. A wood fire glowing in the fireplace at the Bronson ranch was a must almost all year 'round.

Now, how to make contact with that skittish mare? Chasing her was definitely not the way. A horse has to be trained to come when called. But how to train this one whose contact with humans had been so negative?

Lori stuffed a couple of windfalls into her jeans pockets. Would Storm remember the juicy apple she had given her yesterday and have enough confidence to come for this one?

"Here, Storm," Lori called. "Come on, Storm. I've an apple for you. A nice, juicy apple."

The horse listened. But she was not about to come.

"No use to chase her, or even walk toward her," Lori mumbled. "She'd always be a step ahead of me and she can run faster and longer than I can. She's bigger and stronger. I'm supposed to be smarter, though."

Feigning indifference, Lori turned toward the barn. She knew the bin of oats was behind the last stall. Yes, and there was an oats pan. What horse could resist oats? That would bring her running in the right direction quicker than anything.

Back in the pasture, Lori shook the pan so the oats rattled on the metal.

"Hey, Storm! Hear that? Oats! Come on, girl."

There was warmth in the coaxing voice. But Lori wasn't begging Storm to come. She was almost commanding her.

Storm did come. Slowly. She'd come a way, then stop, listening. The sound of the rattling of the oats on the bottom of the pan was intriguing. A plan formed inside Lori's mind.

"I have to be able to communicate with her, somehow," she thought. "I'll teach her to shake hands. I know how. Dad showed me when I first got Patches. Bucky-B could shake hands, too. It only took him a week to learn. If she doesn't think I'm trying to catch her, she'll learn to trust me sooner. I won't bother her head. That makes her suspicious. It makes her want to turn heel and run."

Lori shook the oats pan again.

"Here, Storm, pretty Storm. Oats! Yummy oats!"

Now the two were within touching distance. But Lori just kept shaking the oats pan, holding it out of reach of the mare's muzzle.

She bent over to touch Storm's front right foot.

"Shake!" commanded Lori. "Shake!"

Still sniffing, reaching for a taste of the oats she could smell but not curl her tongue around, Storm actually allowed Lori to touch her right leg. Lori held the oats toward Storm; quickly, the mare lipped a mouthful and began to chew noisily.

"I won't hurt you, Storm. You and I are going to be friends. Want more oats? You can have some. But you have to shake hands, first. Shake! That's right, Storm. Shake!"

Again, Lori touched the mare's right foreleg, grasping it tightly and attempting to lift if off the ground. As a reward for allowing this contact, she was given another mouthful of oats.

By now, Lori felt tired. Having to be alert and tactful was nerve-racking. But exciting and fun. And she had made progress. Real progress.

"Good girl," Lori said, letting Storm clean out the pan.

Lori stood quietly by, speaking in soft tones.

"Here's your dessert. You can have the apple if you take it from the palm of my hand."

Tempted, Storm reached for the apple, but pulled away, seemingly afraid. Her head turned from one side to another, but she never stopped sniffing that apple. It seemed she was almost drooling.

Lori stood patiently. She could wait.

At last, courage conquered fear and Storm

55

grabbed at the apple. She crunched, savoring the sweet juice. Lori longed to stroke the horse's soft nose and velvet-smooth neck. But she would only spoil the bit of confidence gained today. Better leave well enough alone.

"Good old Storm," Lori called, leaving. "I'll be back tomorrow!"

Lori headed toward her bike, keeping her eyes open for Ken. She heard hammering in the barn. What excuse could she think of for going there? The oats pan. She'd forgotten it. She went back to pick it up and was amazed when Storm just stood there. The mare remained alert ready to run. But she did not run.

"Bye, old girl," called Lori, turning back toward the barn.

Ken stopped his pounding. "You're wasting your time," he told Lori. "Even if you ever do get close to her, it's my guess that Storm'll still be a skittish horse. You've taken on a big job. A thankless one, I'd say!"

Lori tossed her head and brushed a black curl behind her ear.

"Wait. Wait and see," she said, smiling as she put the oats pan by the bin. "See any salmon down at the river yesterday?"

Ken's whole face lit up.

"It's fascinating," he said, "the way those humpies batter themselves on the sharp rocks, struggling to get to the exact place where they were hatched three years ago." Ken picked up a nail, held his hammer poised ready. "They've been swimming around in the Pacific Ocean for most of that time. Maybe been almost to Japan or up to Alaska. How they find Puget Sound and then the very stream they came from—well, that's a mystery no one has an answer for. But it's an established fact that that's what happens." Ken resumed his pounding.

Lori knew that if she brought up the subject of salmon, she'd get a glowing response from Ken. Salmon fascinated him, but *he* fascinated her. He wasn't bent on being a football hero. Such an ambition left Lori cold. Ken helped his dad as she had to help at home. In time that was his own, he was tramping river or stream, flushing out grouse, or photographing deer or studying the migratory habits of Washington State's fine resource, salmon.

Lori watched Ken pound. She couldn't understand his intense disgust for that beautiful horse. But that might—just might be to her advantage. It would be if Storm were actually for sale and Lori could, by some miracle, figure a way to raise all the money it would take to buy her.

Ken paused. "Both Joe and Darlene thought seeing the spawning salmon was great," Ken said. "We happened to run into Darlene."

Lori's heartbeat quickened at the mention of Darlene. So she had run into the boys, accidentally on purpose, probably! Lori could just see Darlene's coy smile, the sun glistening on her blond hair as she listened intently to Ken's talk about salmon. Darlene could probably care less. "Smelly old fish," she was thinking, no doubt. Darlene had looks. Darlene had a horse she could jump on and ride to the river just anytime. No helping around the house to hold her back. Some people have everything!

Four-fifty-seven. The voice coming from Ken's transistor radio on the barn windowsill reminded Lori that she'd better get back home.

"See you," she called, hoping Ken hadn't noticed her sudden gloom.

"Wait!" Ken called. "Did you hear about the fire at that old place down by the river? You know. The one with all those apple trees this side of the beaver dam."

Lori paused, waiting to hear more.

"The house is gone. Burned to the ground. We poked around in the ashes but all we found was a blackened teakettle."

"Burned! I liked to prowl in that old house."

"Well, it's too late, now. Arsonists, you know. Somebody's set it on fire on purpose. It's getting to be a habit. That's the third old house they've burned in as many weeks!"

58

Lori shrugged. There wasn't anything she could do about it. This time, as she turned to go, she waved a hand, but said nothing.

Before Saturday, Lori had two more handshaking sessions. It took time and patience. But Lori was so anxious to make friends with the horse with the light mane and tail, that the hours spent in the pasture winning her confidence were pure joy.

But on Saturday, she had to force herself to leave so she could work on that sketch. Of course, she'd had to help give the house a thorough cleaning before she'd been able to leave. The day was wearing on.

Mike wanted to go back on his promise to be a model at the old Jeffrey place. Lori threatened to snatch the poster from his bedroom wall and crumple it if he didn't keep his part of the bargain. That brought him around. Randy had seen it and admired it.

"Why don't you get your sister to make one of you?" Mike asked. "She can draw as good as Lori. Maybe better."

"She's better at making mountains and trees and stuff like that," Randy said. "She can't make people like Lori can, or horses, either. I like this funny kind of people. The picture looks like you, sort of. It's a funny you, Mike. I wish Lori would make a poster of me."

Flattered, Lori made a promise. "I will, some-day, Randy. But I can't right now. Mike can't play with you anymore today. He and I have a job to do. Haven't we, Mike?"

"Where you going?" demanded Randy. "Can I come, too?"

"No, you can't." Lori was firm. She wouldn't have minded Randy's coming, but he might tell Darlene just what her mural sketch was going to be like. If there was anyone she wanted to keep that information from, it was Darlene!

Lori put her drawing materials in Mike's bag, the one he used when he delivered the weekly *Herald* to the rural mailboxes in the area. She set off on foot and Mike went beside on his bike. She could have used her bike, but it irked her to have to ride a bike. If she only had a horse to carry her on wooded paths on a sparkling October day like today! But that was wishful thinking.

Actually, it wasn't far to the old Jeffrey place, a quarter of a mile, maybe. From the window of her upstairs bedroom, she could see the clearing where the frame buildings nestled beyond the orchard. It was past a small lake and across the main road to Roaring Falls. In minutes they were there.

Lori got out her large pad and soft-leaded pencil.

"You'll have to prime the pump," she told Mike. "I want water gushing out. Poke around in the tall grass and find an old can."

Lori eyed the weather-beaten log cabin, the old pump, the lilac bush behind it, the moss-covered wagon wheel.

"There's water in the creek behind the shed," she told Mike. "Just pour water down the pump while you work the handle up and down real fast. Mr. Jeffrey showed me how, once. See if you can get the water up."

Mike didn't want to do what he considered "work," but reminded that this was all part of the bargain, he hunted for an old can.

"This must have been their dump," he called to Lori. "There's cans and bottles here and even an old woodstove. And here's a couple of big rusty milkcans. Come here, Lori. Did you ever see a bottle like this? It's a funny shape. It's blue. A different blue. Come see!"

"Don't bother me with things like that right now," Lori said. There was irritation in her voice. "We came here to do my sketch. Hurry up. Get that pump going!"

Mike did as he was told, but he was in no hurry. He brought a small can of water. It had a hole in it and most of the water had leaked out before he poured what was left down the pump. It didn't do the job and he had to make two more trips to the creek. To Lori's dismay, every time he went, he carried back as many old bottles as he could manage. He dumped them in the tall grass near his bike.

"You're exasperating, Mike! Get the pump going, *please!* How do you think you're going to get all those bottles home?"

"You can carry your old art stuff," Mike informed her. "I'm filling my bags with bottles."

Mike worked the pump handle up and down fast. It squeaked, and almost seemed to groan. At last, water gushed out. Mike worked away at the job he had come to do, fascinated with the stream that flowed in spurts, depending on whether he was pushing down on the handle or raising it ready to push again.

"Perfect!" Lori exclaimed. "Take your shoes and socks off, Mike. I want a barefooted boy. Roll one pants leg up farther than the other. There. Now pump all you want."

Both were so engrossed in what they were doing, that neither of them noticed the old man emerge from the orchard, walking-stick in one hand, an apple he was munching in the other.

"Howdy, young'uns," he called in a cracked voice.

"Mr. Jeffrey! Hi! I'm sketching the old cabin. I asked you if you cared. Remember? You said it was OK."

The old man moved slowly through the tall grass toward Lori, then paused to look over her shoulder.

"Well, I never!" he exclaimed, leaning closer to get a better look with his watery blue eyes. "That kid brother of your'n could be me, Lori. For a fact he could. Many's the time my ma said to me, 'Olaf! Fill the bucket.' She'd need water for dishes or peeling 'taters or scrubbing. Always needed it right now. I learned to get it fast so as I wouldn't get a rap on my head." The old man watched Mike pump. "Where's the bucket?" he asked.

Lori studied her sketch. "You're right, Mr. Jeffrey. Mike's pumping, but we don't know why. Do you suppose there's a bucket on the junk pile? It doesn't matter if it leaks. I just need the effect."

Seeing that it would be a while before the old man could make his painful way to the junk pile and back, Lori put her materials on a rock and scurried over to look for herself. Soon she returned.

"Look!" she called. "I did find an old bucket. There's no bottom in it, but who cares." She held something high. "Look at *this* blue bottle. I never saw one like it. I think I'll clean it up and put it on my windowsill. You don't care if I take it, do you, Mr. Jeffrey?"

"Pshaw, no!" The bewhiskered old man spat. "That's just an old pill bottle. There's probably more if you've a mind to dig. My pa was a great one for pills and linaments. A lot of old-time bottles was blue, you know."

Now Lori's pencil made quick strokes.

"How's that?" she asked. "I'm glad you suggested the bucket, Mr. Jeffrey. Makes all the difference. A horse goes right here just beyond the lilac bush. I'll put her in over at the Silver Spurs. They have a new mare there. A beauty. I want to get the dished face just right."

At the thought of Storm, a sickening feeling overwhelmed Lori. She was getting along so well in being able to communicate. That handshaking trick was working. But the sooner she had the horse gentle and friendly, the sooner she would be up for sale. Ken's attitude didn't seem to be changing. Who would be the lucky buyer?

Lori stared into space, chewing the end of the brown pencil in her hand, when all at once the old shed beyond the junk pile came into focus. At that very moment, a splash of cold water startled her. Mike, laughing, was ready to run when she came after him. But Lori let out a yelp that sounded more like a victory cry than a protest.

"It's hand-split cedar! That old shed and . . . and the woodshed there, and . . . and the chicken house . . . why, they're all weather-beaten cedar. Mr. Jeffrey," she shouted, "you've got a gold mine here! You're rich and you don't know it!"

Bewildered, the old man perked his head sideways so he could catch what Lori was saying with his good ear. Simmering down, Lori dropped to the big rock, her elbows on her knees, her chin in her hands, and explained.

Mike stopped pumping water and listened, too.

"Believe it or not, the city architects are dying to get weather-beaten old hand-split cedar shakes just like those," she nodded to the outbuildings. "I know it for a fact. I was over at Bronsons' when the salesman came. He wanted the Bronson barn, just the barn, mind you, nothing else. He could sell the shakes in the city for the walls of fancy rooms in houses and restaurants. Sounds crazy, I know. But it's true."

The old man ran crooked and bony fingers through his bristling white beard, shaking his head in disbelief.

Lori wasn't finished. "I need money, lots of it, awful bad," she said. She glanced at Mike. She didn't want him to know what she needed money for, so she passed over the part about Storm.

"I can't tell you why I need it. I just do. Do you care if I pull these old buildings apart? We could split the profits. You provide the shakes

65

and I'll do the work. I could get Mike to help me, and maybe Randy. You don't want that old shed or that old chicken house, do you, Mr. Jeffrey? You could use a little money, well, maybe a whole lot of money, couldn't you?"

"They ain't no use to me nor to nobody else, I reckon. I live with my daughter in a fine modern house on the hill. You know that. I just like to wander down here in the orchard and recollect the way things used to be when I was a boy. But this log cabin and all the outbuildings hasn't been used for forty, maybe fifty years. I wouldn't want the cabin touched, but if the outbuildings are any good to ye, take 'em down. You've got my permission."

Mike stuck his freckled pug nose under Lori's face and demanded, "What you so anxious to get a lot of money for? Tell me that! It's got something to do with that horse, I'll bet."

"What makes you say a thing like that, you little busybody? I'm not telling you why I need money. I just do." Lori was defiant. Then her manner softened. "Do you want to earn some, too? If you help me, I'll pay you with part of the money the man pays for the shakes."

Mike was persistent. "How much money do you need? You're going to win that two hundred dollars for the picture you're painting, you know."

66

"Oh, who knows for sure if I'll win? We won't know for a couple of months. If I do win, it won't be enough for . . . well, I need more, that's all. If I don't win, I need all I can get."

Lori gathered up her artwork and was about to toss the old bucket back on the junk pile when she stopped short.

"Where do I sell all this old wood?" she asked, talking to herself. "Do you suppose I can ever find the card the man in the red car gave Ken's dad? Come on, Mike. I've got to stop at the Silver Spurs Ranch before we go home."

"Wait!" protested Mike. "I'm having a hard time getting all these bottles into the bag. Besides, Silver Spurs is past our drive, not before."

"Oh, leave some of those junky bottles here," scolded Lori. "And don't nag at me. I know what I'm doing. I have to look around the barn on the Bronson place."

She tucked one bottle into each of her blue denim jacket pockets and called over her shoulder. "Bye, now, Mr. Jeffrey. You won't be sorry. We'll both be rich—maybe!" Under her breath she said, "I won't be for long. But I'll be able to buy something I want very, very much."

Lori was glad Mike couldn't see the vision in her mind's eye — a spirited but friendly horse, chestnut with light mane and tail.

67

5

A Walk with Ken

MINUTES LATER, MIKE TURNED his bottle-laden bike into the driveway at Marycrest farm. Lori hid her two blue bottles under a fern so she wouldn't have to carry them over to the Silver Spurs Ranch.

"Here," she told Mike. "Take my sketch pad on up to the house."

"How can I? I'm loaded."

"You can carry it that little way. Go on. Tell Mom where I've gone. I'll be back before long. I have to look in Bronsons' barn for a card. That won't take forever."

Lori started jogging down the road, then paused to call, "You don't need to tell about my brainstorm. Let me be the one to tell about selling the shakes. I'll do it at just the right time. Now, keep going with that sketch. Put it on the coffee table where it won't be damaged."

Mike plodded up the hill, pushing his bike, sketch pad under one arm.

Arriving at Silver Spurs, Lori crawled under the split rail fences to get to the barn quicker. Would that business card still be lodged in the crack by the window near the first stall? She remembered exactly where Mr. Bronson had tucked it.

Dusk was settling in. The light in the barn was none too good. Lori couldn't find the card and she was uncertain whether she dared turn the barn lights on without asking, when she thought she heard a voice. Standing motionless so she could listen, Lori took a long breath, then relaxed. It was only Ken. But who was he talking to? As she listened, Lori realized that he was talking on the barn extension telephone.

"Dad's not here right now," Ken's deep voice said.

The sound of the steadiness that stamped everything Ken said or did sent a tingle up Lori's spine. There wasn't another boy in the entire school as — well, as grown up as Ken. No foolishness about him!

"I'm sure he wouldn't mind. Yes, the haymow in the barn would be a good place to hide. But where would you leave the patrol car? Wouldn't that be a dead giveaway? . . . Oh. Sure. That would work. Okay. I'll tell Dad when he comes in from the woods. Sure. Bye."

What was that all about? Suddenly, she felt guilty. She'd been eavesdropping. If Ken came back behind the stalls, he'd find her. Better to make her presence known than to be discovered. Purposely, Lori coughed loudly.

She heard Ken call, "Who's there?"

As he hurried in her direction, he must have seen her form silhouetted against the dusty barn window for he said, "Lori! What are you doing here? You're not training that old nag at this time of day, are you?"

At the same moment, Ken flipped a switch and the stall area was flooded with light.

"Oh, I'm glad you're here. I just had a brainstorm, Ken. I need the card that salesman gave your dad. You know who I mean. Mr. Katz. He wanted to buy the barn just for the cedar shakes he could get by tearing it down. I have to find his address. I just have to!" Lori's fingers explored above the window, then down its sides. "It'd be just about here that your dad poked that card into a crack. Do you remember seeing it?"

"Girls!" was all Ken said, shrugging. Then he added, "Sure, I saw that card. It was there for days, but I haven't noticed it lately. It's probably fallen down and gotten mixed up in the hay and crud on the floor. But why all the excitement?"

Lori didn't answer. If Ken knew how desperately she wanted a large sum of money, he would want to know what on earth for. She wasn't about to discuss that.

"Well, when you're cleaning stalls, if you come across the card, be sure to save it for me," she said.

Changing the subject, Lori said, "I wasn't meaning to eavesdrop, Ken, but what was that all about? Who's coming in a patrol car? Why would anyone want to hide in your barn?"

Ken was sober. "It was the county sheriff," he said. "You know about the fires that are set every Saturday night like clockwork. They're always old abandoned pioneer homes. Somebody has tipped the sheriff off that the house on the other side of the Old Burn Road, here, is the one they plan to set fire to tonight. The sheriff figured if a couple of them could hide in our barn, they might be able to catch whoever's doing it."

"A patrol car on the road would be a giveaway."

"They won't come in a marked patrol car. After dark, they'll come in a regular car and hide it behind the blackberry vines just inside our gate. Then they'll hide in the barn. They'll have walkie-talkies. We may be in for some real excitement tonight!"

"Then, again, it may be very quiet," Lori reasoned. "Maybe it was a false tipoff to mislead the law officers and keep them busy one place so whoever they are can set a fire someplace else."

Ken flashed Lori a grin.

"You've been watching too much TV," he teased.

Lori ignored that remark. "There's a certain magazine article pasted to the wall of that old house that I'd like to have," she said. "It's from a 1929 magazine. I've always meant to pull it off to paste in my scrapbook. I just never did. If there's a strong chance it will go up in smoke tonight, I'd like to go get it now. Want to go with me?"

"Sure. I'll go. I wouldn't want you prowling around over there alone. There's too much junk you could stumble over. Wait. I'll grab a flashlight and turn off the barn lights."

Lori was glad Ken couldn't notice the faint pink that had crept into her cheeks. The warm flush on her face told her it was there. Knowing he cared whether or not she was hurt made her glow all over. Would she dare take hold of his hand when they were in the old house? He'd said he didn't want her to stumble.

Heading for the gate behind Ken, Lori reviewed in her mind the reasons for her having come to Silver Spurs in such a hurry. The discovery of a way to make money fast overwhelmed her. Such good fortune was something she longed to share with Ken. She didn't dare, though. He would only kid her about the folly of wanting the skittish mare he seemed to despise. Still, Lori wasn't sure the horse would actually ever be for sale. If he knew how badly she wanted Storm, he might suddenly take a liking to the horse. Ken wouldn't want to be mean. He wasn't that way. But sometimes people decide they want something just because someone else wants it.

I don't know why, Lori thought, but people are like that.

The flush on Lori's face faded and a chill ran up her back. What if the culprits were planning to set fire to the Jeffrey log cabin and all the outbuildings tonight? Oh, they couldn't! They just couldn't! Not when she had permission to tear off those cedar shakes. She and Mike would have to get right at it. Surely Ken would find Mr. Katz's card. If he didn't, there'd be some way to trace him, someone to call who could give her a clue how to find him. A real estate office. That was it. She'd do some phoning on Monday. She'd hope and pray that the arsonists would leave the old Jeffrey place alone.

"Watch where you go!" Ken said. "Don't trip on the vines coming up through the floor."

He flashed the beam of the light in his hand first onto the floor, then onto the walls.

"Which article were you after, Lori? Remember where it is?"

"It's a story about the early history of this area," Lori said, reaching for Ken's hand to steady herself on the uneven boards. The feel of his hand in hers brought that glow back to Lori's cheeks, she could tell. Her brown eyes sparkled triumphantly. Darlene could ride her horse to the river to see Ken accidentally on purpose, but had she ever been in an old abandoned house at night with him? Hardly!

"What was the history about?"

"It told how the people who settled here around 1840 or 1845 got together for a potluck dinner on a Sunday. The women talked about all the mice in their cabins. One said she had a cat and not one mouse. She agreed to lend the cat around to the different cabins for a few weeks at a time. She made everybody promise to take real good care of it. So that's what they did. I thought it was a cute story, that's all. Especially since it really happened."

Ken's toe hit something. There was a bump, bump and a thud. He spotlighted the object and picked up a bottle.

75

"Weird shape," he said and was about to toss it back to the floor, when Lori caught his arm.

"Give it to me," she said. "I'm a bottle collector. Started today. I found two blue ones over at the Jeffrey place."

Lori clapped her hand over her mouth. Would Ken ask what she had been doing over there? Well, she'd been sketching. But if he knew, Darlene might worm the information out of him. She couldn't let Ken know about the rivalry and jealously that flowed between the two of them. She was sure Ken didn't really know Darlene like she did.

"Mike and I were exploring along the stream that leads to the Jeffrey cabin," Lori hastily explained. "We found a junk pile and Mike went home loaded with old bottles. At first I scolded him. I'm a typical big sister, I guess. But I found a couple of blue bottles I really liked, so I stuffed them into my jacket pocket. If I take this bottle, I'll have three for my windowsill. When I wash all the dust off them, they'll sparkle and look kind of nice, don't you think?"

Ken nodded. His eyes scanned the wall.

"Is this it? Is this the article we came after?"

"That's the one!"

Quickly he pulled the page from the wall, gave it carefully to Lori, then put his hand on her elbow to help her down the rickety steps.

"You can't go home alone in the dark," he said. "I'll walk you home. Then I've got to hurry back. I haven't told Dad about the call from the sheriff. I want to be around just in case something interesting goes on."

Lori longed to be in on the action. But no one knew for sure if there would actually be any. Besides, the officers might hide in the barn until three in the morning or longer before anything happened.

Lori didn't walk her fastest. She wanted to savor the deliciousness of being escorted home in the dark by Ken as long as she could. But there had to be an end.

"I hid my bottles under this fern," she said, stopping and feeling for them. "Here they are. Now I have three pretty bottles, thanks to you."

They neared the house. "Thanks for walking me home. Mom'll be glad. Be seeing you."

Lori turned, her hand on the knob, and Ken called "G'bye," as he took long steps back down the driveway.

The crunch of Ken's shoes on the gravel road was all she had to remind her of that hour with Ken all to herself. Usually, she had to share him with people or horses or cows . . . or his beloved salmon. But this time he'd done what was important to her. No, the crunchy sound, now nothing but a whisper, wasn't all. In her hand she clutched the ancient magazine sheet he had found for her and folded so carefully. And she had a bottle with unusual markings. She could feel the raised writing on the bottle and wondered what it said. She'd find out in time. Right now, she had her mother to soothe. Mom would be edgy because she was so late.

It's a good thing she doesn't know why I have to find that card left by Mr. Katz, Lori thought. If she knew I could actually see my way clear to having another horse, she'd object. She's so fearful when it comes to horses. But it's for Dad's good I want Storm, as much as for myself.

6

The Destructive Mr. Midget

LORI GAVE HER MOTHER a peck on the cheek, something she'd been neglecting to do lately.

"I like your perfume, Mom. And say, I'm sorry I'm so late. But don't worry. Ken walked me all the way home. He had a flashlight."

Mrs. Goodman sighed. "I wish you wouldn't worry me this way, Lori. How did I know you were with Ken? You know as well as I do how strangers like to park on the Old Burn Road. Please don't let it happen again!"

"Yes, Mom. But didn't Mike tell you where I went? I gave him my sketch and told him to tell you." Lori raised her voice. "Hey, Mike! Where are you? Where's my sketch? I want to show it to Mom!"

Mike came bounding down the steps two at a time. His face was one big storm cloud.

"Have you seen Mr. Midget?" he demanded. "He's not in his cage. In fact, he's not in my room. Period. I've searched everywhere."

"Cool it," Lori said. "He'll show up."

"I even looked inside my slippers in the closet. And in the sleeves of my sweaters and shirts. I just can't find him!"

"He's probably behind the pillows on the davenport. Or chewing a tunnel through some old newspaper. Look in the woodbox by the fireplace. By the way, Mike, where'd you put my sketch? I keep asking and you don't answer."

"I put your dumb old sketch on the coffee table in the front room like you told me to." Mike was yelling, almost hysterical. Losing Mr. Midget was a tragedy that no one was taking seriously.

Anxious to divert her mother's attention, Lori headed for the coffee table. They could discuss the sketch. Her mom had good ideas, sometimes, about balance and design.

Lori turned on the front room lamp, then let out a yell.

"Mike! Here's your bratty ratty varmint! And just look at what he's done! Chewing newspaper, my eye. He's chewing my sketch. Scat, you rat!"

Mike made a dive for the davenport, reached behind the pillow and came up holding onto Mr. Midget by the tail. Mike ducked to avoid Lori's hand. Intending to strike Mike, her fist hit the table instead and she screamed in pain, then burst into tears.

"My sketch is ruined! It took me all afternoon, too. There's hardly enough picture left to tell what was there!"

Lori sank to the davenport and buried her head in her arms on the coffee table.

"What's going on in here?"

Even before he spoke, the sound of footsteps had told Lori that her dad was coming from the basement. She wiped the tears from her eyes with the back of a hand, ashamed of the violent outburst. She knew that loss of control was a disappointment to her dad. He was a patient man. She could see that in his good left hand he carried a lamp base.

"I want to show you that I'm not completely helpless," he said. "Look what I was able to make on the lathe. It's a new lamp for your room, if you want it, Lori. If I take time, there are a lot of things I can do. Believe it or not, I can even pound a nail with my left hand. Can hold onto the nail with these two fingers sticking out from the cast. . . ." He paused. "Oh. That's the trouble. Mr. Midget chewed your sketch."

81

Lori peered with misty eyes, trying to fit frayed pieces together.

"There's the log cabin, the barefoot boy pumping water into a pail, the lilac bush — it's not as badly chewed as you first thought, Lori. You can look at this and redo the sketch. It'll take a little time, but all is not lost. Chin up!" Mr. Goodman put his left hand on Lori's chin and turned her face up toward his so their eyes could meet. "There are worse tragedies in life than a chewed-up sketch."

"Do it over! What good will that do? How do I know the new sketch won't get chewed up?"

"Keep your art work in your room."

"Are you kidding? My room's next to Mike's. If that dumb gerbil got loose once, how do I know he won't do it again?"

Lori rested her chin in her hands, staring straight ahead.

"What I need is a studio. A place that's all my own where I can go to my drawing. But that's just a dream I've had for a long time and won't ever get. Chewed. My sketch is all chewed."

Mr. Goodman's face brightened. "I've got the solution. Why didn't I ever think of it before? Are you listening, Lori? I think you'll go for this."

"I'm listening."

"There's a part of the loft in the barn that we aren't using. By putting up just two partitions, I could make a cozy little studio for you. You could do all your artwork there. Mr. Midget isn't likely to find you out there. How does that sound?"

"Oh, Dad! Do you mean it?"

Lori jumped up and threw her arms around her father's neck, careful not to jar the arm in the cast.

"You mean the part where that old round-topped trunk is, don't you?" Lori said. "I could clean up the trunk and put my sketches in it. Only how could I keep warm? I couldn't do my best if my fingers were cold."

"We'd wire an outlet for an electric heater. Maybe we can find a potbellied stove for when you expect to be there a while. There's nothing nicer than the warmth from wood burning in a fireplace or stove. We have plenty of alderwood."

Lori laughed right out loud. Her mind raced, exploring possibilities.

"I'd have a really modern studio," she said. "The old rough barn walls are the rage in the newest houses. Did you know that?"

When her dad shook his head, no, she went on, "It's true. There's a man who buys old cedar shakes just for new 'rec' rooms and restaurants. And you know what, Dad? I'm going to be rich! Old Mr. Jeffrey promised me I could pull the shakes off his outbuildings. We're partners. I get half for doing the work. I might even pay Mike and Randy to help me. I heard about all this at Bronsons'. I have to find out where to sell them. But that's a minor detail."

"Say! That's great!" her dad responded. "If you're able to earn money like that, you can buy your own shoes. And maybe that sweater you've been hinting for. Making the studio for you won't cost much. But that might be a way to buy the wire and the stove. I'm proud of you, Lori. . . ."

Lori's face sobered. "I didn't exactly have shoes and wiring and a stove in mind when I made this deal," she mumbled. She looked up at her father. "But how is this building project going to be done? You can't build with one arm."

Her dad picked up the lamp base for an answer.

"I told you if I take it easy, I can do quite a bit. Jerry called me just today. Wanted to know if I could make him a deal on firewood. He's mighty handy with a hammer. He can wire, too. This may be the kind of deal he'd go for. The two of us could get it done real fast."

"You're wonderful, Dad!" Lori gave her father a kiss and moved on to the kitchen to show the pieces of the sketch to her mother and to see if there was something that needed doing toward supper.

The next morning, Lori hoped to arrive at Sunday school early so she could hear about any excitement that had gone on at the Silver Spurs the night before. But Mr. Midget was on the loose again and by the time he was back in his cage there was just time to drive to church for the opening service. Lori did manage to pass a note to Ken during the singing. His eyes met hers and his lips formed the words, "Nothing happened," as he shook his head.

Lori got the message. It had been a false tip. At least, the pioneer house on the Old Burn Road was still standing. That gave Lori a start. She was singing but she was thinking, "Let's hope the firebugs bypassed the old Jeffrey place."

In a moment, Lori relaxed, remembering that she could see the outbuildings from her bedroom window. If there had been a fire there, she surely would have known it.

By the time the Sunday dinner dishes were done, Lori was anxious to prowl in the barn, thinking and planning for her new studio. A lot of old stuff was stored in that loft above the place where baled hay was now stacked for the cattle. Dressed in her oldest jeans and a denim jacket, Lori poked in spite of dust and cobwebs and pulled out an old table, an ornate door, the round-topped trunk, and she even found a kerosene lamp stored in a box, complete with lamp chimney. She'd buy kerosene to have light to draw by if the electricity ever went off in a storm. Neat! She'd ask her mother for a crocheted rug or two. And what about those bottles? They'd be just right to put on the windowsill. They'd add sparkle and color. She could see it all.

It would be great. Just great! Now if only her dad could hurry or at least get help in putting their ideas into reality. After all, the days were ticking by. That sketch had to be completed and submitted all too soon. Darlene probably had her design planned for the library mural and maybe ready to turn in. But then, Darlene's life was uncomplicated. She already had her own horse. She hadn't bargained to spend an hour every day training a horse that wasn't hers, and might not ever be. She didn't have the worry of having to try to earn several hundred dollars — just in case. Lori found herself wondering just why she did spend all that time on Storm. She'd laughed at Mr. Bronson when he asked how much she was going to charge him. So it wasn't for money.

It was a challenge! Yes, that was it. Could Lori really gentle this horse? Mr. Bronson had believed she could. She had to prove his confidence in her was justified.

Lori wiped the back of her hand across her forehead to push back a curl that tickled her head, leaving a dusty smudge. Actually, things were looking up. With a place all her own she might come up with a sketch that would win the coveted prize money. If not, there was always the cedar shake money. Mike and Mr. Midget had done her a good turn, after all. Without that chewing episode, who knew? She might never have had the prospect of her own studio.

Yes, things were looking up.

7

Lori's Loft

THERE WAS LITTLE LORI COULD DO about the studio until her father and Jerry, the neighbor who had consented to help, had the partitions up and the door in place. They decided to put in a large picture window, too.

"I've a piece of plate glass collecting dust in my garage," Jerry said. "What good is an art studio without good lighting? You can give me an extra cord of wood to settle the score. That'll be for the window, installed. Like the idea?"

Lori and her dad thought it was a bargain.

Mr. Goodman worked at the project during the day. Jerry came to help after supper. The men strung up a light with a long extension cord, joking and laughing as the work progressed.

"Dad is beginning to sound like his old self," Lori thought as she swept up shavings one night. "This project is a challenge. He has a feeling of satisfaction, even if he is slowed down, having only one hand to use." She dumped shavings from the dustpan into a box. "I don't think the old sparkle will be back in his eyes until he's on a horse again, though. A horse he can trust. No use talking to him about maybe getting Storm. He'd just say something about Mom's fearfulness and not wanting to worry her. Mom's so neat in so many ways. If only she didn't have that big hangup about horses!"

No. This horse problem was one Lori would have to work out without even consulting her father.

That all-important hour Lori spent daily with Storm was paying dividends. Mr. Bronson surprised Lori as she worked with Storm one day. She'd been so intent on what she was doing she hadn't noticed Ken's dad shortcut from the woods to the house. He stood still, gaping.

There was Lori, facing Storm, but bending forward.

"Shake!" she commanded.

The horse actually raised her front right leg, let it dangle relaxed from the knee, and allowed Lori to grab hold and pump it up and down as she "shook hands."

It wasn't until Lori offered Storm an apple for reward and was stroking the velvet-smooth neck that Lori noticed she had an audience.

"I'm dreaming," exclaimed Mr. Bronson. "Don't wake me up, Lori."

Lori giggled. "We're communicating, Storm and I. We shake hands to show we're friends. She doesn't try to get away when I put my arm around her neck. In fact, I half believe she thinks I have hold of her and that I'm in charge."

"I can't believe you've made that much progress in so short a time!"

"Of course, she could break and run any moment. She probably would if I had a rope in my hand. One of these days I'm going to hide a halter behind my back. While she eats oats, I'll slip my arm around her neck, then a soft rope. I think I can get a halter on her. Then things will be a lot easier."

"Halter? Where's the halter she wore when she first came? You grabbed her by a lead rope that day in the barn. Remember?"

"She must have rubbed it off in the woods, Mr. Bronson. I've never seen a halter on Storm after that barn-kicking incident. But she'll soon know what a halter is, and a bridle and bit, too. Won't you, old girl?"

"Don't try to mount her unless someone is right there with you," cautioned Ken's dad. "If she should buck you off, you might need help in a hurry. That's a rule when breaking a horse. You'll remember, won't you?"

Lori nodded. "Please don't tell my dad what I'm doing," Lori reminded him. "I want to surprise him. Can't you just see the look on his face when I ride up to Marycrest on this horse? I've made up my mind to buy her, Mr. Bronson. That's if she's still for sale."

Lori smiled when the farmer nodded that the horse was.

"I can pay for her, too. That is, I'll be able to do it in a few weeks. Mike and Randy and I spend every chance we get pulling shakes from the outbuildings over on the old Jeffrey place. Remember Mr. Katz?"

"Sure do."

"I couldn't find the card he gave you, but I called the Northwest Realty in town and they gave me his phone number. He's sending a truck out a week from Saturday right after lunch. I won't be trying to ride Storm until after that.

Mr. Katz is in a hurry. There's a restaurant going up north of here and they're just about ready for our shakes."

"Seems strange Olaf would let you tear those buildings down."

"He won't let me touch the log cabin. It has shakes only on the lean-to, anyway. But he doesn't mind the woodshed and chicken house being torn down. He has a good place to live with his daughter, but he likes to have money he can call his own. It's nice for both of us."

Mr. Bronson nodded agreement.

"And say, Mr. Bronson. I'll be paying cash for Storm in two or three weeks. Only is it all right if I leave her here until she's really trained? I'll probably have enough to buy the feed, too. It's just that I want to surprise my folks at the right time. You know. Wait until she's gentle and well behaved."

Surprise? No need to tell it the way it was. Shock would be a better word, at least as far as Mom was concerned. Oh, well, she'd get over it when she saw Dad's contentment astride the prettiest horse in the county.

Lori didn't see Ken very often these days, much less talk to him. She couldn't skip the training sessions, even if they were short. But there was never any time to linger because she had a date to meet Mike and Randy after they grabbed their snacks. Boys always think about food, especially right after school.

It was surprising how much the two got done. Lori had borrowed her dad's crowbar, without mentioning to him that she was taking it. She showed the boys how to pry the shakes loose, one layer at a time, without breaking them, then put them in neat stacks.

Those piles of shakes were like money. Soon they'd be the means of making Storm her very own. Mr. Bronson said so. It was as good as done, almost.

Then there was the sketch. One Wednesday after school, Lori went up to inspect the progress on her studio. A handcarved nameplate on the door made her gasp. LORI'S LOFT, it said.

Her dad, hammer in hand, paused to enjoy his daughter's reaction to his original touch. Lori was in for another surprise behind the door. Her dad had gone to an auction and bid on a pot-bellied stove. Secretly, he and Jerry had installed it. There it was, complete with a glowing fire. Since it was now the end of October, the warmth radiating from the big black stove was welcome.

"It's just too wonderful!" Lori laughed. "You're the best dad I ever had!" She gave her father a hard squeeze that almost made him lose his balance.

"Glad you like it, Lori," he said. "The zinc sheet for the stove to stand on came with it. Nice, eh? Now you won't have to worry about sparks popping out the door and setting the barn on fire. The asbestos sheet in the back was my idea. It doesn't look so good, but it's an extra safeguard. Keeps the stove from being a fire hazard."

Lori's dad glanced at the drawings tacked to the wall. "Now, sketch away," he said. "I'm counting on you to win that prize!" He went back to his hammering.

Lori had already hung a calendar. It pictured a mare, surprisingly like Storm, only with dark mane and tail, standing over her newborn foal. It was a tender scene.

"Why not?" Lori thought. "Why not breed Storm and let her foal? In time, Dad and I could each have our own horse. And what horses!"

But this was no time to dream. Lori had looked at the calendar to check just how many days before the sketch was due.

"Halloween's tomorrow. Then two more weeks. That's the deadline. I must get the sketch redone to where it was before Mr. Midget took over. Then I have to use Storm for a model and draw her into the picture in just the right place."

Lori was overwhelmed with a feeling of panic.

There was so much to do and so little time to do it in.

The next day, Ken seemed to be slowing his pace from the house to the barn so Lori could catch up with him as she hurried to put the oats pan back.

"Going trick-or-treating tonight?" he asked, a little embarrassed, Lori thought.

She shook her head. "I can't, really. I have to work on my sketch. I was slowed down when Mike's gerbil chewed my picture to bits. Besides, I thought maybe I was getting too old for that!"

"That's what I thought," Ken admitted. "Haven't been for several years. But Darlene said everybody was going this year. They'd dress up crazy and it was a good way to get a bunch of candy."

Lori had to think quickly. She'd already committed herself by saying she had to draw, and she did. But she couldn't let Ken go trick-or-treating with Darlene, even if a bunch of other kids would be along, without getting into the act somehow.

"Tell you what," Lori exclaimed. "Make your last stop my new studio in the barn. I'll ask Mom if it's OK, but I'm sure she won't care. The studio is in the loft above the baled hay. You'll see the sign on the door: LORI'S LOFT. I'll have a snack ready and you guys can share the goodies you get trick-or-treating. It will be sort of a housewarming for my studio. How does that sound?"

"Great! Just great! It's a deal. I'll steer the gang over Marycrest-way around nine-thirty or ten."

Ken took the oats pan from Lori and she called good-bye as she hurried to crawl under a fence and be off to the old Jeffrey place.

The work of lifting the hand-split cedar shakes was nearly done. Lori was glad because she had invited company and didn't know if she had anything to serve. Fortunately, there was plenty of cider. Her dad had kept the windfalls picked up and cider was a logical use for them. Popcorn! That's what she'd have. If she had a good fire in the potbellied stove, one of the boys could make popcorn in a deep skillet on top. She'd melt butter in a pan on top, too. Lori brought the big kettle from the house, and paper cups and napkins.

"Have fun!" her mom called as Lori went out the door. "I'll poke my head in once or twice to see if you need anything.

"Thanks, Mom!"

Lori did a little on the sketch, but very little. She was too excited, wondering when the gang would burst in. She had to have her sketch tucked safely inside the round-topped trunk to keep it away from Darlene's inquisitive eyes.

After lighting the kerosene lamp, Lori turned out the lights. Lamplight and the glow from the stove gave the only light in the room.

The bottles on the wide windowsill sparkled. Bottle collecting had turned out to be a fun hobby, after all. She would poke around in the Jeffrey junk heap as soon as the shakes were delivered and maybe find more. Why, the truck would be there tomorrow! Lori sighed with relief. It had been a long hard job, longer and harder than she imagined it could be. But it was worth it. How else could a high school sophomore earn so much money? For Storm, Lori'd do any amount of work!

Shivers ran up Lori's spine at the thought of the way Storm had rubbed her arm with her muzzle that very afternoon. Lori could still feel the softness of Storm's lips, exploring her hands, then her face and hair.

Mr. Bronson sure was surprised to see us shake hands, Lori thought. That's only the beginning. Just wait until she lets me mount. Just wait until she lopes with me on her back, thrilling to the power beneath me. And just wait until Dad goes riding! That'll be the day!

The sound of the fire crackling inside the stove reminded Lori that she was expecting company. She stood still, listening. Were they coming? It was almost ten. The swinging pendulum schoolhouse clock, another of her dad's auction bargains, said so.

There was the sound of feet mounting the steps to the loft, but it couldn't be the gang. They'd be bounding up with a whoop and a holler.

Lori opened the door.

"Ken!" she exclaimed. "Are you alone? Where's everybody else?"

8

Up in Smoke

KEN SHIFTED THE GUITAR CASE from his left hand to his right and paused to admire the old-fashioned lantern, wired with electricity, that lighted the steps to Lori's loft.

"Dad haunts the auctions." Lori laughed. "That's one of his treasures. Like it?"

"Sure do!"

"Come on in. See the potbellied stove he got me."

Ken entered the loft behind Lori.

"The rest should be here before long. I think I heard them coming up from the other end of the Old Burn Road."

In answer to the questioning look in Lori's brown eyes, he explained. "No, I didn't go trick-

or-treating like Darlene wanted me to. I had to go to Lonesome Creek to measure the velocity of the water so I can make a report to the Fisheries Department."

"You went to the creek to do what?"

"Oh, didn't I tell you? I'll explain about it some other time. Anyway, it takes two people and Dad couldn't go with me until late. So I called Darlene. Told her I couldn't make the trick-or-treating part, but I passed on your invitation to end up at the loft."

"What did Darlene say to that?"

"She said she'd tell the others. I think she said, 'Good! I've been wanting to see that famous loft of Lori's I've been hearing so much about from Randy.' Anyway, they should be here, soon." He held out his hands to the warmth radiating from the stove. "It's nippy outside tonight. The fire feels good."

Lori opened the trunk lid to find a poster-sized tablet and leaned it against the wall where it would be handy. She had an idea, but it was a surprise. On impulse, she picked up her sketch and held it up for Ken to examine.

"Like it? Tell the truth, Ken. Do you think it'll be chosen for the library mural?"

Ken's mouth dropped open. "I knew you could draw, Lori, but I didn't know you were that good."

102

Lori glowed at Ken's unrestrained admiration. "A horse goes in this spot," she said. "I'm going to use your Storm for a model."

She heard the tramp of feet thundering up the steps. Hastily, Lori put the drawing into the trunk and banged the lid shut. There was a brief knock, then in they trooped: a bunch of mustachioed desperadoes, Indians, bums and gypsy girls.

It was easy for Lori to recognize Joe, with Darlene hovering close behind. (Good, thought Lori. You stick with Joe and leave Ken alone.) Next came Gibson, Dave, and Shorty who called to Debbie, Joan and Pam to hurry up. Lori laughed at Pam's jack-o-lantern.

"Set it on the bookcase, why don't you?" Lori said.

She counted noses. "Nine came. Great! Look around all you want, gang, then grab a pillow — they're Mom's contribution to my new loft — and find a place to sit on the floor. Ken brought his guitar. We can sing."

"Your loft is great," gushed Darlene. Was there envy in her voice? "You should be able to win the prize, with a place like this to work in. By the way, do you have your sketch around?" She scanned the loft wall where Lori had tacked samples of past work. "How're you doing on it, anyway?"

"Oh, it's coming along," Lori answered. She was purposefully noncommittal.

The trick-or-treaters compared the contents of the pillowcases they had used as sacks while collecting loot. Gibson commented that his can of pressurized shaving cream was empty.

"I really decorated the yellow car parked in the power line right-of-way where it joins the New Burn Road," he boasted. "I don't know who would park there this time of night. There's nothing in any direction but the old Jeffrey place. Nobody'd have any reason for going there."

When Ken started to strum his guitar, kids settled on pillows on the floor, munched candy bars and apples and began to hum as Ken's deep voice led out. He knew old songs, funny songs, Negro spirituals. He murmured something about how would they like to hear a song he'd made up himself.

Gibson swung the stove door open so they could see the glow of the fire. The light from the kerosene lamp flickered, making eerie shadows on the walls as Ken sang slowly, sadly, questioningly.

Lori sat in the background. She had picked up her tablet and pencil and sketched with quick strokes. She listened to the words.

"What's life all about, anyway?" the singer asked. He described the major and minor crises that beset a person from the cradle to the grave.

"Is this all? Is there more?" he asked.

To Lori's satisfaction, Ken did answer the questions that haunt every thinking young person. "Yes, God, our Maker, wants to be your Friend." The words of the song told how.

"The messages we hear at church every week have really gotten through to Ken," Lori thought. She was proud of him. Her church life was a vital part of her total week, too. "Nobody'd guess it, though, the way I blow my top sometimes. And the things I think about Darlene." Lori stole a hasty glance in Darlene's direction, glad it was shadowy dark in the room.

Ken switched to a song in a lighter vein, one in which all could join. While they sang, Lori moved from the back, over to the wall near where Ken sat and tacked up the sheet of paper she'd torn from the tablet. Everyone stared at the drawing, trying to discern it in the dim light. As they took in the fact that the bold outline was a perfect caricature of Ken sitting there strumming his guitar, they burst out laughing and applauded.

Bewildered, Ken turned to see why they laughed. Then he laughed louder than anyone.

"It's yours," she nodded to Ken. "Take it home with you."

A change of pace was needed.

"Who wants to be in charge of the skillet on top of the stove?" Lori asked. "We need to fill this kettle with popcorn. How about you, Gibby?"

Gibby agreed, and he went at it as though he'd done it before.

"I want to try hypnotizing someone," Lori said, raising her voice to be heard. "Who will it be? How about you, Ken?" She tried not to sound obvious about wanting her partner in the act to be Ken. "Mind stepping outside? I'll get my den set up and call you in a minute."

Ken left, grinning. Quickly Lori borrowed Pam's gypsy headdress, snatched two saucers from where she'd set them earlier on the wide windowsill and held a lighted match to the bottom of one. The rest watched, wondering. Plopping two big pillows on the floor, Lori called, "Come on, Ken. Come back in."

Ken came.

"There. You sit opposite me and do just as I tell you."

Lori handed Ken the saucer with soot on its underside.

"I'm about to hypnotize you, Ken Bronson. You are getting sleepy," Lori intoned. "You are relaxed. You and I are alone. No one else is here. You have no mind of your own. You will do just as I do. You do just as I tell you to do. . . ."

Lori's low voice drifted on and on. All the time she was rubbing her right forefinger around the bottom of the saucer, then rubbing it on first one cheek, then the other, back to the underside of the saucer, then on her chin and forehead. Ken was copying her. Soon there were giggles and guffaws as the members of the group saw what was happening. Ken was being tricked into smearing soot all over his face.

"There's a mirror on the back of the door," shouted Debbie. "Ken, go look at yourself."

Ken looked, then he doubled up, laughing.

Lori removed her scarf and glanced toward the window as she did.

"What's going on?" she gasped. "Hey, gang. There's a fire. Is somebody burning brush?"

Lori answered her own question. "The arsonists are at it again! It must be the old Jeffrey place. Oh, no. . . ."

"Come on, everybody," called Ken, bounding down the steps. "Maybe we can catch them. Maybe we can put out the fire or call the cops or do something!"

Gibby took time to empty his pan of fluffy white kernels into the kettle before dashing out to catch up with the others. Lori was too shocked to move. The sky was so bright she was almost certain that her piles of weather-beaten shakes were being consumed in flames.

Quickly, Lori pulled herself together. She dashed down the steps and across to the kitchen door to fling it open and call to her folks.

"There's a fire at the Jeffrey place! Call the fire department! Call the sheriff. It's probably the same guys that set the other fires!"

Lori saw her mother head for the phone. Then she banged the door shut and ran, breathless, to catch up with the others.

She was overwhelmed by the sense of loss. The trucks would have come tomorrow to haul away the valuable shakes. But the culprits, whoever they were, had changed their pattern of striking only on Saturday. Because of Halloween they had burned a pioneer place on Friday this week. And they had chosen the Jeffrey place!

"It can't be," Lori protested in a singsong chant as she raced along. "It can't be. Oh, it just can't be."

But she knew it was only wishful thinking. As she neared the old farm site, her fears were confirmed. Standing around the piles of burning shakes, the shakes she and Mike and Randy had worked so hard to remove so carefully, was a bewildered group of mustachioed desperadoes, Indians, bums and gypsy girls.

Flames danced skyward, far above the heads of the spectators. Besides the crackle of the flames, Lori detected a familiar sound. The squeaking of the pump. That was it. She looked. Ken was pumping water and Joe was carrying a large old milk can. Miraculously, the log cabin was still standing!

"Mr. Jeffrey will be glad," Lori whispered. She ran over to ask if she could help. Ken told her to hold the second rusty milk can steady while he pumped furiously. In seconds, Joe was back to pull the full can out and replace it with the empty one. He sloshed water in his haste and Lori's right foot was shocked by the cold. She pushed the curls from her face with the back of her hand, and grabbed hold of the other milk can to steady it.

The next time Joe returned, he called to Ken, "That's enough. We've saved the cabin. I can't see any more fire. There's no use to tackle the other fires. They were too well under way before we left Lori's."

Ken mopped his brow with a red handkerchief. "Thanks, Lori," he panted. "You helped. It might not seem like much. But every second counts in an emergency."

There was the low rumble of a car engine and suddenly the entire scene was illuminated by brilliant spotlights. The revolving blue dome light on the car told them that the sheriff had come.

Ken stepped forward. "I'm Ken Bronson."

Ken glanced at the rest of the gang, realizing suddenly how comical everyone looked in his Halloween get-up.

"These are all good guys," he confided. "We were having a little party in Lori's loft over at Marycrest—you know, the house on the knoll north of here—when we saw the flames from the window."

"Did you see anyone leaving?" one officer asked.

The other kids gathered around, listening. Gibby pushed to the front and blurted, "We didn't see a soul. But earlier when we were passing the Power Line road where it meets the New Burn Road, right down there," he pointed, "I saw a yellow sports car parked. I had a can of shaving cream and I decorated the car, but good. Squirted the gooey stuff along the hood and sides in stripes. I emptied my can on it. We were headed for Lori's and I figured it was the last car I'd see. It was, too."

"Yellow sports car, you say? Did you notice the year, the make or the license plate?"

Gibby scratched his head. "It was already dark," he said. "Still, Pam had a jack-o-lantern along and when she came close I did notice that the three letters before the numbers spelled the word POP. 'It'd be an easy one to remember,' I was thinking. Yep, that was it: POP. That help you any, even if I didn't notice the numbers?"

"Well, it's a clue, a pretty good one, at that. The first three parts of the license, the color of the car, the fact that it was a sports car and one smeared with shaving cream . . . you've given several clues. Of course, they could wipe the cream off. Probably did that the first thing."

The two sheriffs turned on powerful flashlights and looked around. Ken spoke up again. "Joe, Lori and I doused out the blaze in the log cabin, here."

Joe nodded.

"It took fast work and a few cans of water. These milk cans, I mean. But we got it out."

The officers pushed past the boys. "We'll check for burnable material. Stuff the guys might have used to start the fire in the cabin."

A quick search of the one-room cabin turned up oil-soaked rags, charred and soggy. One officer picked them up for evidence.

"Better clear out of here," he told the young people. "We'll want to inspect it by daylight and we won't want anything touched. We're glad for the clues you've given."

"Go back and finish your party," the other officer said, "G'night."

Back on the road, the group talked in hushed tones for a while, speculating about the arsonists, and the chances of finding them and the punishment they might expect. Finally, Debbie spoke up. "I'd like to go back to the loft, Lori, but I'd better not. It must be getting late and my folks'll be expecting me to show up pretty soon. I had a good time, though, and thanks a lot!"

"Mom will take you home," Lori said. "Come on. She doesn't like girls out in the dark alone. Joe, you better come, too. You live way over by Debbie. The rest of you guys can make it on your own. Right?"

As Lori had said, her mom was glad to drive the kids home. There wasn't room for Lori to go along, though. It was just as well. She wanted to be alone for a while.

Slowly she climbed the steps to the loft. She blew out the kerosene lamp, then moved to the window. She hadn't noticed the moon before, too many clouds, perhaps. Right now the moon was shining out from under black clouds. Across its face rose wisps of smoke, lingering reminders of a dream gone up in smoke.

Lori sank to a pillow on the floor and let the tears flow unchecked.

"I was so sure," Lori sobbed, "so sure that Storm would soon be mine, bought and paid for in full! And now she's not. She's not mine at all. I have no money. Not even any prospects of getting money."

Lori switched on a light. She lifted the top of

the trunk and taking out the sketch, studied it.

"Is this going to be the stepping-stone to my getting two hundred dollars?" she wondered out loud. "I have to win that prize, now. I just have to! But will I?"

Lori opened the door of the potbellied stove and stirred the coals with the poker. The flames leaped up, fell back and shadows danced across the caricature of Ken still tacked to the loft wall.

For a moment, the warmth of the early evening washed over her — Ken's coming early, his delight over the loft, her relief that he hadn't gone trick-or-treating with Darlene after all, the joy of hearing him sing in those firm deep tones, a worthwhile song he had written himself.

Now, Ken's laughter as he spotted the picture Lori had drawn of him still rang in her ears. He'd been a good sport about that soot all over his face. Had the officers noticed? Oh, well. They wouldn't think much about it. After all, it was Halloween and he had been fighting a fire.

It was a Halloween to remember! It was a day when Storm had shaken hands willingly. Lori had thought of her as saying, "Hello! We're friends, aren't we?"

Instead, was Storm shaking, nodding a goodbye?

9

A New Business

IN SPITE OF THE OVERWHELMING ACHE in her heart and the feeling of futility, Lori continued to work with Storm each day. Grooming became one natural and easy way of making friends. The horse now trotted across the pasture when called by name, crunched the apple offered on a flat, upturned palm and willingly shook hands on command. She even stood patiently, allowing the green nylon halter to be slipped over her head and fastened. It was no trouble for Lori to snap the soft cotton lead rope to the halter, either.

The two would trot around the pasture, the girl holding lightly to the lead rope at the left side of the horse's head. A few times, at first, Storm had refused to be led. Lori knew that pulling and yanking at an animal heavier and stronger than she was not the solution. So she tried a trick she'd read about. Grasping the lead rope firmly, assuming an "I am in command" attitude, Lori led Storm in circles. Around and around they went three times, pivoting in a small space. So confused was Storm by this unusual procedure, that when Lori led her straight ahead, she had forgotten what she was being stubborn about and went right along.

Ken's chores of caring for his dad's beef cattle meant that he was in and out of the barn. The horse no longer spooked at being tied in the stall. Ken could go about his business of cleaning stalls while Lori brushed and curried, using a hard rubber curry, rather than a metal one. Such harshness on the Arabian's sensitive skin would have sent her hind feet flailing again.

The firm, but not too firm, circular motion of the rubber currycomb seemed to feel good to the horse. As the currycomb became full of dust, Lori would tap it against the wall. Even this noise did not disturb Storm for, before each use, Lori would allow the horse to look at the currycomb and sniff it. This satisfied her curiosity and removed the fear of the unknown.

Lori was especially careful of Storm's beautiful flaxen mane and tail. Knowing that a hair can be broken in a moment and that it takes months to replace, she painstakingly removed as many tangles with her fingers as possible. Then, using a stiff-bristled brush, she started at the roots of the mane and forelock, brushing every bit, even the underside of the mane that did not show. She used the same brush for that long swishy tail, starting at the tip and gradually working up toward the dock so she wouldn't overlook one snarl.

So far, Lori had not yet tried to put a bridle and bit on Storm, nor had she tried to mount her. That time would soon come. At present, Lori was content with thorough grooming and exercising as a means of developing mutual confidence. Even the act of lifting each of the mare's feet, one after the other, to inspect the hooves for possible stones and to clean the frog with the aid of a hoof pick, was a way of helping horse and girl to understand each other.

Sometimes, Storm didn't want to cooperate with the daily hoof inspection. Lori would run her hand firmly down the back of a foreleg from the knee to the fetlock. If Storm didn't pick up her hoof, Lori would lean the weight of her shoulder against the horse, shoving her slightly off balance, and up would come the hoof.

Ken, pushing a wheelbarrow past, paused to compliment Lori for the way she and Storm were getting along. Lori looked over the side of the stall and flashed a grateful smile at Ken. She was flattered that he admired her way with his horse, but inwardly, she felt threatened. Even though at the moment she had little hope of being able to raise the amount of money she'd need to buy Storm, if Ken fell in love with the horse as she had, there'd be no Storm to buy.

"She'll probably turn out to be a good horse after all," Ken conceded. He picked up the handles of the wheelbarrow. "But an Arabian, at best, is still an Arabian. Give me Rowdy, any day! Too bad he's not for sale. I don't know how many times I've teased Joe to sell him to me. But he always says, 'No go.' And that's that!"

Well!

It was now the first of November, and there was an urgency about finishing the sketch. Lori brought her art work along to the Bronson barn. She now had the new sketch she'd copied after the gerbil had gone on a chewing spree. Lori,

perched atop a stack of baled hay, used Storm as a model as the horse stood in the stall munching hay.

Lori had been forgetting to bring Ken the caricature she'd done that fateful Halloween night. She made sure she had it this time, so he would have to come to her and maybe talk about her drawing. She needed to hear him praise her work. It would bolster her self-confidence. Winning that honor and especially the prize money, was now a consuming passion.

Ken looked at the drawing briefly, but he had told her before that he liked it. There wasn't much more he could say. Fearful that he might take off in a hurry, Lori said, "You promised to tell me what it is you have to do at Lonesome Creek once a week. Is it the Fisheries Department you're doing it for?"

Ken climbed up the bales of hay, ladder-like, and sat down beside Lori. She kept her eyes on the horse, then her drawing, then back to the horse. There was a glow on Ken's face. She knew by the tone of his voice.

"I was following Lonesome Creek, the one that flows out the lake over by the Jeffrey place, when it came to me that this would be a good stream to plant fingerling trout in. The State Fisheries Department does that, you know. That's what some of the money they collect for fishing licenses goes for, for fingerlings to grow into adult trout for fishermen to catch. Anyway, I'd never seen trout in that stream. So I wrote a letter to the head of the department, no less. And guess what!"

"What?"

"I got a letter back saying my deductions were well founded and that the field representative would contact me and inspect the stream with me."

"Did he really do it?"

"He sure did. But before stocking the stream, he wanted to know the depth and the speed of the flow of the water week by week. That's to make sure the stream doesn't sometimes dry up so much that all the trout would die. So guess who's elected to take a reading once a week until spring!"

"Three guesses? The first two don't count!"

"Anyway," he went on, "I've got my work cut out. But it's fun work. It takes two. You drop a leaf into the stream and at that moment I have to look at the second hand on my watch. When the leaf rides the water to the second stake, you call out 'Now!' and I check the watch again. Of course, it all has to be written down. Want to go with me?"

"Just let me know the next time you have to go."

"You'll need boots. It's marshy underfoot in places."

Ken was on the barn floor in one leap and back to his work with a cheery, "Be seeing you."

Lori wrapped up her drawing and headed for home on foot.

Waiting for her beneath the stairs that led to her loft were two young boys. As her foot touched the third step, they dashed out at her and said, "This is a stick-up! You have to promise to make a picture of all our friends, or we'll kidnap you!"

Lori screamed in mock fright, then laughed.

"Get along, you two," she ordered. "I haven't a spare moment. Do you realize how close that deadline is?"

She pushed the door to her studio open with a foot, removed the drawing from its wrappings and held it at arm's length. Mike and Randy pushed close to get a good look. Hastily, Lori covered it, remembering she didn't want Randy, of all people, to see it. But it was too late. He'd seen. So she held it up again. The admiration of both boys was loud and genuine.

Lori cautioned, "Don't either of you tell anyone about my drawing. You understand? It's a secret until it's been judged." She eyed Randy. "Don't tell Darlene. You hear?"

"Don't worry," Randy said. "If Darlene asks

I'll say you keep it locked in your trunk."

"You'll win, Lori. You're sure to win!" This from Mike.

"The judges might have other ideas!"

"It's finished, isn't it? What else do you have to do?" Randy asked.

Lori studied the drawing.

"Why, I guess you're right, Randy. There isn't much more to do, now that the horse is in. If I fuss with it, I might spoil it. Now all I have to do is write a two-hundred-word essay telling why I think my drawing should be made into the mural for all to see in the library. That won't take me long."

"Good!"

"Hey, that's great!"

Mike and Randy began to sock each other in mock fighting as an expression of their joy. Lori would have time to do as they asked, after all.

"We have a plan. We want to invite our friends to come up here to the loft so you can make a picture of each one. A funny picture, the kind you did of Mike with Mr. Midget." It was Randy talking.

"You don't have to do it for free, Lori," added Mike. "Punky and Ginger and Dave and Ricky and Bernard — they've seen mine and everybody wants one. We told them it would cost two dollars each. But they said they didn't care."

"They all have money saved from birthdays and some have grandpas that give them dimes to save, or all their pennies, so they get cans full of them. You might be paid in pennies."

"Will you do it? That's what we want to know!"

Lori laughed. "I guess I will. My drawing is done and . . . and there's no work at the Jeffrey place. Say! How many kids can you round up? I'll give you a quarter for every customer. That way you'll make money and I'll make money. Do I ever need it! Even if I win the prize, I need more money. This is as good a way to start as any!"

Mike asked slyly, "Could you need money for a horse, Lori? You know how Mom is. Scared of a horse's shadow." Mike's voice was high and singsongy and teasing. "Better not get your heart set on Storm."

Lori struck at Mike and missed on purpose.

"You just be quiet, Mr. Smarty Pants. When does the first customer come?"

"In half an hour! Wait right here!"

"I'll be in the kitchen. I'm sure I'm supposed to do something toward dinner. But come get me and I'll slip back up for a picture or two."

The boys dashed down the steps.

"Do I need the money," Lori mumbled. "Do I ever!"

10

The Final Sketch

To LORI'S AMAZEMENT, the caricature business mushroomed. Randy was delighted with the impish life-size picture of himself. He ordered two more and Lori gave him a bargain price of three for five dollars.

"I never know what to give grandparents for Christmas," Randy explained. "You know that old advice about doing your Christmas shopping early. Well, that's what I'm doing!"

A few days later, Lori demanded, "Randy, have you shown Darlene the picture I drew of you?"

"She's jealous! She wishes she could do as well, but she can't. Oh, she can draw, but she can't draw funny people the way you can, Lori."

Randy and Mike both earned quite a few quarters by bringing in customers. There were always those who tagged along to see what was going on and often they'd make appointments for the next day. Gibby's little sister was fun to do because her hair was in pigtails and she had an oversized mouth she wore in a perpetual grin. She liked to talk.

"Guess what!" she said. "The sheriff came to our house. It wasn't very exciting, though. All he wanted to know was what kind of shaving cream Gibby used when he went trick-or-treatin'. Once he took Gibby away in the patrol car and I thought that would be fun. But Gibby said he didn't do anything but ride to the power line so he could show just where the yellow car was. The sheriff looked in the mud to see what the tire tracks looked like."

Lori gave Karen stale popcorn left from the Halloween party that had been interrupted by the fire. If she was busy eating she'd sit still and stop talking. Lori hoped the arsonists would be caught. Thinking about the whole mess made her sick in the pit of her stomach. She wished she'd never even found out about those weather-beaten shakes being worth so much money.

Karen said she was bringing her grandpa to have his picture drawn. Only she didn't know if he'd want it done. She said she would bring him up to see the loft and Lori was to draw his picture real fast when he didn't know what was going on.

On Wednesday, when Karen said they'd come, Lori was surprised to hear a familiar voice in the barn below. Opening the door, she saw Mr. Jeffrey mounting the stairs, painfully and slowly.

"When Karen said she was bringing her grandpa to see my loft, I didn't realize she was bringing *you*, Mr. Jeffrey! I'm glad you've come."

As the old man stood on the top landing, breathing hard, Lori studied his face, deciding what features she would emphasize to characterize him. The hooked nose and stubble chin, the lined face and pale eyes — his would be an easy portrait to do. She helped him settle in her round captain's chair to study the drawings on her wall; then she quickly picked up a thick pencil, and, with deft strokes, began to get his likeness onto her pad.

Karen kept up a steady chatter with her grandfather, discussing the various pictures to hold his attention. Then she had a sudden inspiration. She caught Lori's eye, motioned toward the trunk, raised her eyebrows in a gesture that plainly said, "May I show *the* sketch to Grandpa?"

Lori nodded yes. After all, what she hoped was her prize-winning picture was of the cabin in which the old man had been born.

His eyes lit up when he saw it.

"There it stands! Big as life! That's me, pumping water for my ma. I kin hear her hollering yet, 'Olaf! Get a move on. Get that water into the tubs on the stove. It's bath night, you know!' I'd pump till my arm was like to fall off. Still, them was the good ol' days. 'Course I had to chop wood to keep the fire in the cookstove goin'. There was always somethin' that needed doin'. It seemed like a lot was expected of me. On the other hand, I don't think anything tastes as good nowadays as that fresh-baked bread, hot from the oven, with some of my ma's strawberry jam."

Lori's hands were busy while the old man reminisced. Karen danced back and forth to see how things were going. The grin on her face showed that she was pleased.

"And that horse," Mr. Jeffrey went on, "is mighty lifelike. You done a good job, Lori. You're sure to win the prize. I'm one that will be right on hand to congratulate you when they call you up to hand it to you. But say, what horse is this? One over at the Silver Spurs?"

Lori nodded.

"Times has sure changed. Silver Spurs! It's mostly a cattle-raising farm these days. Time was, they had the finest Arabians in the county, maybe the state, foaled on that very place. That was before Bronson moved in. The name stuck,

Silver Spurs, that is; but there hasn't been a horse there for some time. Whose horse is it? Bought for young Ken, was it?"

"Well, yes. Storm — that's the horse's name, was bought for Ken. But he doesn't take to her. Right now, I'm doing the training. Mr. Bronson asked me to. Storm and I are getting along fine, too!" Lori's eyes lit up. "You should see her shake hands and come when she's called and trot along beside me. Pretty soon, I'm going to be riding that mare. I'll come up to your place and show her to you on one of our rides."

Karen hopped on one foot, then the other at the old man's delight when Lori presented him with the portrait of himself.

"Well, I never!" he kept saying.

With Lori's help, Mr. Jeffrey rolled the picture and tucked it under his arm. Then she helped him descend the stairs from the loft.

"I'm due over at the Silver Spurs for my daily training session," Lori said. "But come back again, sometime, Mr. Jeffrey."

After calling to her dad from the kitchen door to let him know where she'd be, Lori hopped onto her bike and took off. She was backing Storm out of the stall when Mr. Bronson came into the barn.

"Oh, it's you, Lori. I hoped I'd see you today. I've seen you putting a saddle on Storm lately.

Trying to get her used to it so someday you can get onto her and start riding her, I suppose."

"She's about ready for it, don't you think?"

"You've done real well, Lori, communicating, as you call it. That handshaking bit was a brainstorm. You've come a long way, but skittish as she was, I'm afraid for you to mount her — not until a real horse trainer has had a few sessions with her."

It was impossible for Lori to hide her disappointment.

"I know you wanted to train this horse all by yourself," Mr. Bronson went on. "But it's better to be safe than sorry. I'm afraid she hasn't forgotten how those boys treated her."

Lori opened her mouth to speak, but Ken's dad kept talking.

"Don't want her bucking you off, Lori. I don't want to have to phone your dad with the news that Lori has a brain concussion from the way she landed when Storm let loose."

Lori leaned against Storm's sleek side. The horse reached around and with rubbery lips explored Lori's shoulders, neck and hair. It was purely a friendly gesture.

Lori had been waiting for the day when *she* could trust Storm enough to mount her. Now she wouldn't be allowed to — not until someone else had done it first.

"Who you going to have break her?" Lori finally asked. "It costs money to have a horse broken by an expert."

"You're right. It costs a heap — usually. But Bill Granberg will work on her every day for a week, longer if he needs to, if I haul hay for him. He bought a barn full of hay on a place over on the Tolt road. If I move it to his barn, it's a deal, he says. Ken can help me on Saturday. He might grumble a little, but he'll have to help." Mr. Bronson moved to leave, then paused. "I suppose you're wondering why I'm willing to go to this trouble on a horse Ken doesn't care for."

Lori nodded.

"Well, I've been toying with the idea of keeping this horse for my own use. Rode a lot when I was a boy. Might just enjoy it again."

Lori gulped. Was Storm going to be available to her, or wasn't she?

"'Course I'm just toying with the idea, as I said. No matter who owns her in the end, she can't be broken any younger. So I've made this bargain. I won't be out anything but my time. Besides, if I decide to sell her, I can add to the price."

Lori gulped again. Add to the price? She couldn't even see where the three hundred and twenty-five dollars was coming from. Oh, well. She wasn't going to worry about that now.

"I can lead Storm down there and she won't even have to be taken in a van," she said. "I can watch, can't I? When do you want her taken?"

"Saturday. Before noon."

And so it was, that on Saturday morning, Lori whizzed through the housecleaning and escaped before her mother could think up extra jobs like giving the stove a thorough cleaning or going through a closet. Walking down the hill, holding Storm's lead rope in both hands, there was a certain lightness in Lori's step. The day before had been the deadline for handing in the sketches for the proposed library mural. That project had been of primary concern to her for a long time. Now there was nothing to do but wait for the judges' decision.

On the way to the library to submit her sketch to the librarian, Lori caught sight of Darlene coming from the other direction.

"Oh, oh. Too late to duck and hand my sketch in later," Lori breathed.

The two girls arrived at the library door at the same time.

"Hi, Lori. Going to take out a book?" Darlene laughed. By what each carried, it was obvious that this was a moment of climax of weeks of work.

Lori smiled, not too enthusiastically.

"May the best one win!" Darlene said.

It just might be you! Lori thought. No question about it. You can draw. "We'll know next Friday!" she said.

Now, Lori quickened her pace to keep up with Storm.

The Fall Festival was scheduled for the day after Thanksgiving. The highlight would be the announcement of the contest winner. A knot formed in Lori's stomach and her breathing became faster at the thought of it. She'd have to figure out what to wear, just in case she actually did win a prize and would have to walk in front of all those people. Ken would be there, of course, and Mr. Jeffrey, and all the kids from school.

There wouldn't be many in town who didn't come. In the time between, Lori would concentrate on learning just what a "pro" did to break a horse. She'd have to think up some good excuse to be away from home. Well, maybe not. It wasn't too far past the Silver Spurs. The biggest problem would be to keep Mike from discovering what was going on and blabbing it to the family, when Lori had her turn on Storm.

As she opened the Granberg gate, she saw Mr. Granberg working out a horse in the training arena. A short beep on a horn announced the arrival of Ken and his dad with the first load of hay.

By the time the hay was in the barn, Mr. Granberg was ready to take over with Storm's first lesson in accepting the burden of a human body on her back and being happy about it.

"With her history of abuse as you've described it to me," Mr. Granberg said to Ken's dad, "there's a certain risk in mounting her. But it's the kind of challenge I live for. An animal as fine as this one is useless, except for breeding, until she is broken to the saddle. Just let me get a cup of coffee and I'll take her on."

Ken and his dad joined the trainer for coffee in the tack room, but Lori stayed close to Storm, stroking her and talking in low, comforting tones.

"You mind the man, Storm. The more you object to what he wants you to do, the harder it will go for you. You're going to have to mind in the end, Storm. Be a good horse and learn to obey real fast. Do it for my sake, will you?"

Standing there in the chill November air, warmed slightly by thin rays from the sun, Lori stamped her feet to stimulate circulation. The warmth from Storm's big body felt good and the sleekness of her hide reflected Lori's good grooming. Lori had the feeling that after their days of getting acquainted and acquiring confidence in each other, the actual mounting would be a simple next step. She still felt a little resentful that Mr. Bronson had taken this part of Storm's training out of her hands.

Lori's thoughts were interrupted by the coming of the trainer along with Ken and his dad.

Mr. Granberg took the lead rope from Lori, and began to talk to the mare. He unhooked the halter and slipped it down around her neck, then coaxed the bit into her mouth. He pulled the mare's ears through the straps of the bridle, then adjusted her flaxen mane. Now, reins in hand, he led her toward the arena.

"Wish me luck," the trainer called over his shoulder. "This old girl may surprise us with a good bit of action. Then, again, she may not."

He opened the arena gate, let Storm through, latched it behind her, then stood on her left side, close to her head.

Lori and Ken both moved toward the white fence and climbed onto the bottom board.

"This ought to be good," breathed Ken.

11

Bucking Bronco

LORI WOULD SOON KNOW if Mr. Bronson had been justified in giving this part of Storm's training to an expert.

"I'll need your help, Bronson," Mr. Granberg called.

Ken's dad climbed the corral and joined the trainer.

"Hold her head, will you? I'm going to put my weight on her back to see what she does. Hang onto her, now. Keep her under control!"

Cautiously, the man threw the weight of his body across the saddle. Storm danced, side-stepping nervously. Bill Granberg slipped down, spoke softly to her, then repeated the process several times.

"Get behind the fence now, if you will," he told Mr. Bronson. "I'll mount her and see what happens. Training an old horse with bad habits isn't the same as breaking in a young horse. It isn't a step-by-step process, slow and sure. I may have to be pretty persistent to show her who's boss!"

Ken's dad handed the reins to Bill Granberg and joined Ken and Lori. The trainer had the reins over the horse's head. He pushed the flap of the saddle back while he tightened the girth. The stirrups were in place.

Storm's ears pointed back, then forward, and her long neck turned so she could see what was going on.

Now the man gathered up the reins in his left hand, then placed it on the mare's withers. With his left shoulder against Storm's left shoulder, he lifted his left foot toward the stirrup, talking quietly to the horse all the time.

"Steady, old girl. You and I are friends, you know. You're taking me for a ride. A nice smooth ride. No bucking-bronco stuff, you hear?"

Storm must not have heard. The moment the trainer swung his right leg over the saddle, before his foot had time to feel for the stirrup, she was indeed a bucking bronco!

With neck arched and rump high, her rear feet flew out in fury. Next, her whole body lifted into the air and she came down to earth on all fours, stiff-legged, in an attempt to jolt this foreign object from her back — now!

The trainer, clutching the horse's mane, anticipated the next bucking maneuver and he was ready. With a sudden shifting of his weight, he threw the horse off balance before she could leap skyward a second time. Each attempt to rid herself of the man on her back was thwarted by the way the rider leaned. Apparently, he was anticipating her moves, for he stuck with her. But the mare hadn't given up yet.

The lump in Lori's stomach was one big painful knot. Instinctively, her left hand moved across the top fence rail and felt for Ken's hand.

"Oh, Ken!" Lori sucked in her breath as the horse continued to fight for her freedom. "Settle down, will you?" Lori pleaded. "Be a good girl, please. Don't throw him. *Please!*"

Ken grinned. "What do you expect of that fool Arabian? Crazy as they come. This is better than the rodeo at the County Fair. And all for free!"

Mr. Bronson stood behind the two, his fists clenched, all attention. Breathless, the three spectators waited.

In moments, Storm struggled for a free head, but the trainer, aware that the reins gave him the advantage, kept her head up. In that position, her attempted bucking action fizzled out.

Storm stood still momentarily, nostrils distended, eyes rolling, blowing and snorting.

The three at the rail fence waited, expectantly. The trainer sat alert, hoping to anticipate the mare's next move.

What the spectators saw was just like a movie rerun. Bouncing, bucking. Flailing hooves. A stiff-legged jolt.

Again, Storm stood stock-still, then shook her entire body in a gigantic controlled shiver. Was she going to yield?

When Ken nudged Lori and pointed to the prints her fingernails made in his palm, she withdrew her hand, stuffing it and the other into her jacket pockets.

The rider dismounted, stood patting the horse's smooth neck, talking quietly to her.

Lori breathed hard. Was Mr. Granberg going to mount Storm again?

He was!

Surprisingly, Storm stood still. Her rump swayed from side to side as her rear feet danced a bit. But her front feet stayed in place, more or less. There was no bucking, no jumping into the air and landing on all fours, stiff-legged. One ear was laid back close to her head. But the other ear was forward, a sign that the mare was aware of the man on her back and that she knew he was boss. She seemed to know that she must try to understand what *he* wanted.

"She's learning," Lori whispered, clenching her fists. "Good for you, Storm! You're learning."

Lori hated to admit it, but Ken's dad had known what he was doing. Without an expert's showing the mare who was boss, Lori could have been hurt, perhaps seriously. Her dream of having Storm for her very own, her dream of seeing her dad riding happily once more, would have been shattered. She sent a grateful glance Mr. Bronson's way.

Storm was prancing a little, but she wasn't bucking — yet. Hopefully, she had learned her lesson. Mr. Granberg sat for what seemed a long time, though it was probably only minutes, talking quietly to Storm, patting her neck.

Then slowly, very slowly, he swung his right leg across her rump and dismounted, dropping lightly to the ground. In his left hand he still held the reins. Storm's ears twitched this way and that. It was as though she were questioning what this determined creature expected of her. He offered an apple on the flat of his hand, one he pulled from a jacket pocket.

"That's enough for today, old girl," he said. "We've both had enough. But we'll try again tomorrow."

Mr. Granberg wiped his brow with a red bandanna. Then he laughed, releasing nervous tension. Ken and Lori scrambled over the fence when he gave the nod and Lori took the reins. She led Storm around the ring at a brisk walk to cool her. Then Ken opened the gate so Lori could lead the horse to a stall. Storm would be staying at Granbergs' for however long it took her to learn the lesson she had come for.

The trainer and Ken's dad lingered to discuss the mare's performance, but Ken followed Lori.

"It's like I said all along. What can you expect from a fool Arabian?"

"She's smart! She'll learn. She learned a lot just today, didn't you, Storm? You'll see. I'll be riding Storm soon, maybe next week. She's going to be such a dependable saddle horse I could even ride her in the parade!"

Lori surprised herself by this last statement.

"You wouldn't!"

"Why wouldn't I?"

"You couldn't!"

"Why couldn't I?"

"The Pioneer Days celebration is less than three months away! That horse? Take a rider through a crowd in that short a time? You've got to be kidding, Lori!"

Lori led Storm into a stall.

"If I'd trained her by myself, yes. But by this time next week Storm'll have learned more than I could have taught her in a month. Or maybe ever. Arabians are smart whether you think so or not, Ken. And *this* Arab, well, she's something else, again. Aren't you, Storm?"

She picked up a brush to groom the mare, removing sweat and dust from her chestnut coat.

Later, Lori made sure the latch on the stall clicked as she turned to leave the large barn with Ken.

They had to pass a long row of stalls on the way back to where the men were still talking. Some stalls were empty. Others housed horses

143

Mr. Granberg was either in the process of training, or boarding for people from the city who
liked to ride but who had no place to keep a horse
except at a stable.

The two peered into the stalls as they passed.
Ken paused before one where an Appaloosa was
looking out inquisitively, munching hay con-
tentedly.

"Now, there's a man's horse! Reminds me of
Rowdy. I wonder if this one's for sale. Some are,
you know. When people have a horse to sell they
often ask Mr. Granberg if he knows of a buyer.
I think I'll ask him. There's no harm in that."

Lori shook her head. That boy! One minute
he ridicules the best horse in the world, the next
minute he's interested in an ordinary-looking old
horse with spots on its rump!

"Indians rode Appaloosas," Ken said. "Can't
you see them charging across the plain? Shooting
buffaloes or chasing an enemy. The breed almost
died out, but it's popular again."

"Looks like an ordinary horse to me."

"The more spots on the rump, the more expensive the horse. 'It shows good color' is the
way they describe that kind of horse. This one
costs plenty with such distinct spots. You can
be sure of that!"

"I couldn't care less!"

"Some horse-lover you are!"

Lori laughed. "Oh, Ken. You know how many hours I've invested in Storm already. You can like any horse you want. Just give me Storm!"

"Give you Storm! You already act like you own her!"

Lori glanced at Ken. Was he kidding her or was he jealous . . . or what? She wasn't sure she liked his attitude. She wasn't even sure he liked her.

They were nearing the end of the row of stalls. It gave Lori an excuse to break into a trot toward the men so Ken couldn't see her frustration.

"Storm will be ready to go in the Pioneer Days Parade, won't she?" she asked the two men, then added, "Oh, excuse me. I didn't mean to butt in."

They both smiled and began to ponder her question. Mr. Granberg shrugged.

"With the right kind of handling when I'm finished with her, there's a possibility!"

Ken's dad grinned. "His opinion is worth more than mine. I liked that mare the first time I set eyes on her. After watching today's performance, I like her even better. 'Course I'm glad it's Bill, here, and not you or me, who's doing this early breaking-in. But when he's finished and with what you will be able to do, I'm likely to have a riding horse that's the envy of every serious rider in the county!"

There it was again! The threat that Storm wouldn't be for sale if and when Lori earned the money!

Lori felt limp. The excitement of the past hour had drained her strength. The frustration of not knowing how to take Ken was getting her down. Of her feeling toward him she had no doubt. There were times in the past when she felt the feelings were mutual. Today, well, she wasn't sure.

Lori was glad when Ken's dad called to him that they better be getting that second load of hay before stopping at the house for lunch. It gave her an excuse to ask when the next training session would be so she would be sure not to miss it, then head up the winding Old Burn Road toward home. She needed to be alone. She needed to walk rapidly, giving the thoughts in her head a chance to sort themselves out.

There was the gnawing uncertainty about whether her drawing and essay would win the contest, and the worry about how to add money to the slowly growing bank account.

True, it had taken a sudden spurt when the boys started bringing candidates for poster portraits. To date, Lori had banked forty-two dollars on the deal — more than she'd made picking strawberries and this was easier and faster. It was a fantastic idea for Christmas gifts and folks were beginning to be frantic about their shopping.

What about babies? She hadn't done any babies yet, and that was sure to be a potentially good market. Maybe she could beg a spot near the entrance of Dudley's Department Store, inside where her fingers could stay warm. It would attract customers to the store and earn money for her. Yes, that was a possibility.

Better work hard and fast. Better not count on the prize money. It had certainly been an education to watch Mr. Granberg handle Storm. Lori gulped. What if she had tried to be the first to mount Storm instead of Mr. Granberg? Even when the trainer was through with Storm, could the horse be trusted? Lori could still see Storm shake and shiver, snorting.

Suppose Storm, by some miracle, were hers for keeps? How would her folks react? Her dad would be no problem. But Mom, as sweet and understanding as she usually was, had a fear about horses that made it impossible to reason with her. Besides, with the burden of working in town and still keeping a well-organized household, her take-it-as-it-comes disposition was suffering.

Lori quickened her strides. She felt guilty. She was always trying to figure ways to zip through the jobs assigned her, instead of planning ways to do them a little better. She had become an expert, lately, at finding valid excuses for putting things off. She kept the dishes done up. Yes. But the kitchen cupboards were streaked with cooking grease and fingerprints. Her mother kept a shelf full of the proper cleaning agents, but now that she was working, hardly a bottle had been opened.

Lori would have loved to retreat to her loft, build a glowing fire in the potbellied stove, and take out her frustrations by drawing whatever came into her mind. A snorting horse. A bare-branched tree, brown leaves burying its feet, lonely arms reaching heavenward, aching for companionship. Shaving cream streaking back and forth across a yellow sports car, shaving cream streaking down the road, into a wooded path right up to the arsonist's hideout. She, Lori, would receive a handsome reward for finding the burners of pioneer homes; homes which were loaded with memories, last links with the past.

But no. She'd better get at those cupboards. Her mother might faint from shock. Lori would risk that. She could still think, scrubbing. Like what was Darlene's drawing about? Was it well done? What chance did Lori's sketch have against Darlene's?

Of course, thinking about it wouldn't change a thing, but the busier she could keep, the faster time would go.

12

Waiting and Worrying

WEDNESDAY AFTER SCHOOL, Lori boarded the
school bus and found a seat by a right window,
hoping she might catch a glimpse of Storm as
the bus passed Granbergs'.

At last it was here — the beginning of the
Thanksgiving vacation. The day after tomorrow
she would know. There would be the holiday
dinner to worry through and the next day would
be *the* day! The great Fall Festival, climaxed
with the announcement of the contest winner.

Above the hum of the bus motor's being
warmed up, Lori was aware of Darlene's voice. It
was more high-pitched than usual, rambling on
and on. She put her own thoughts aside and
listened. Although both used the same bus stop,

Darlene never sat beside Lori anymore. Darlene was almost always certain to see that she found a place beside Ken who boarded the bus early and who always found a seat by a window in the rear.

"Visiting Lori's loft gave me an idea," Darlene said as the bus lurched forward.

"What kind of idea?" It was Joe's voice. Good. Darlene must have found the seat beside Ken taken, so she settled for Joe.

"I told Dad I wanted a studio all my own, like Lori's, only nicer with knotty pine walls. Dad said, 'Sure. I'll have Nils come over. Tell him what you have in mind. I'll write the check.' "

"That's great!" Joe said. "Where'd you put your loft?"

"It's not a loft," retorted Darlene. "It's a studio. It's upstairs in the old carriage house with a breezeway between it and the house. I can cross in any weather and not get wet. It was a natural. Dad's antique Model T Ford is just below and beyond are the horse stalls."

"I ride Rowdy a lot, even in cold weather, but I never see you on Pokey. Don't you ride anymore?"

"I'm getting fed up with old Pokey. She's a good kid's horse, but I'm not a kid anymore. I need a more spirited animal."

Lori shifted her position. Darlene already

owned a good horse and now she wasn't satisfied! Lori breathed hard. If only she had had a horse, the horse of her choice! Darlene complaining! What next?

She didn't have to wait long to have her question answered.

Joe prodded, "You really buying a new horse?"

Darlene bubbled on. "Why not? When Dad came out to inspect the studio Nils and I dreamed up, I mentioned wanting a better horse. He just said, 'Find the horse. I'll write the check.' Good old Dad! He's not around home much, except on weekends. But I can have just about anything I want if I handle it right."

Probably tired of Darlene's boasting, Joe must have tapped Ken on the shoulder, for Lori heard Joe say, "Hey, Ken, did you hear that? Darlene is horse hunting. Wants a spirited animal. Know anyone who has one for sale?" Joe laughed, knowingly.

Lori gasped. No, Joe, no! Don't suggest anything like that!

Ken answered Joe, but Lori didn't hear what he said. She did hear Ken's deep rich rolling laugh and, as always, it sent her heart skipping. Lori relaxed. By laughing, Ken had no doubt silenced Joe's suggestion.

Darlene seemed intent on getting one more point across to her male audience before the bus came to Ken's stop.

"Guess what! I'm planning a party for right after the festival Friday night, a sort of celebration . . . well, that is, someone will be announced winner of the art contest, and well, whoever it is will be invited, of course, and we'll have fun. Will you come, Joe? Ken, I want you to come, too. Will you? Consider this a personal invitation!"

Lori couldn't hear what Ken said. If only she had sat further back in the bus today. She could have watched the three as they talked. She couldn't risk giving away the fact that she was listening to every word by turning around. Perhaps Ken only nodded.

Some nerve! Darlene didn't come right out and say so, but it was plain that she expected the celebration party to be in *her* honor!

Was she that sure of winning the first prize? The nails of Lori's right hand dug deep into the flesh of her left hand. For a long time, she'd envied Darlene's poise and self-confidence. This was egotism with a capital "E."

Lori had time for only a glimpse of Storm before the bus driver ground into second and started the slow ascent up the winding hill. After the bus stopped at Silver Spurs, Darlene and she moved toward the front, waiting for their stop.

Before the two parted, Darlene said, "I'm horse hunting. Did you know? I hear Mr. Granberg is doing a great job in breaking Storm. That horse sure has the class and looks I'm after."

Darlene tossed her head, eyeing Lori for the effect her next remark would make.

"I'm going to ask Mr. Bronson if he'll sell Storm to me. It won't matter about the price. Dad promised to write the check when I found the horse I want."

Lori gasped. Darlene smiled smugly.

"Not Storm," Lori blurted. "That is, you're not likely to find her for sale. Mr. Bronson told me he likes her more every day. Aims to keep her for himself. . . "

Lori hated hearing her own words, because that meant that Storm would never be hers, either. But it made her see red to think that Darlene could consider having Storm for *her* horse!

Darlene paused another moment before starting down her driveway.

"Well, he might be persuaded to change his mind. Money talks, you know. I'd just love to ride her in the Pioneer Days Parade!"

"Be seeing you," Lori mumbled as she took off toward the house on the hill.

Lori was unenthusiastic about the holiday dinner preparations. Always before, she'd been delighted over the smell that filled the house when the oven door was opened at turkey-basting time. Polishing the good silver, getting down the sparkling crystal that was used only on festive occasions, making place cards — all these things used to be fun.

Now, she went through the motions mechanically. There'd be company, of course. She would force herself to be polite and live through the day, somehow.

It seemed the only bright spot in Lori's life was the fact that the cast had been removed from her dad's right arm. His spirits were high and it made her feel better, even if she was sort of numb all over. He still favored the elbow, for normal use was returning slowly.

Monday, he'd see how things went at the shop. Life at the Goodman house would eventually be like it was before the accident. That was a comfort.

Since the next day would be *the* day, Lori excused herself, after dishes were done, to go to her room. She wanted to make sure her clothes were ready. She had decided to wear a turquoise wool. It was a hand-me-down from a cousin, but it was her favorite color, the color she felt good in. Somehow, the brilliant blue was the right compliment to her olive skin and black hair.

Studying herself in the mirror in a trial dress-up session, Lori decided that even if she didn't win the coveted prize, she had to look her best. The eyes of a lot of people would be on her, waiting to see her reaction when the prize winners were announced.

On Friday evening, she picked at her dinner, then excused herself to dress. If only she weren't so nervous!

So much depended on the evening's outcome. Besides the honor of being chosen as the artist worthy of doing the library mural, Lori needed the prize money. She didn't have a father who could say, "Pick out your horse. Let me know and I'll write the check."

Then there was that party in Darlene's studio. In case Darlene was the winner—and she seemed so sure of herself—would Lori be invited?

The witch! Snooping around in her loft to get ideas, then having her own studio made by a professional! Knotty pine paneling, yet!

Would Ken go? He'd wiggled out of trick-or-treating with Darlene. But that had been several weeks ago. She'd been working pretty hard on him ever since. She latched onto Joe just for that evening, then dropped him until Wednesday on the bus. That was the kind of person Darlene was. She used people. That was it. She used them, got them to do what she wanted so she would look or feel better.

Lori glanced into the mirror for one last self-appraisal. The scowl on her face startled her. Who'd be attracted to a grouch like that?

Besides, she was supposed to be happy. She'd soon be standing in front of that vast crowd accepting congratulations and the envelope containing the prize money.

Or was that wishful thinking?

13

The Judge's Decision

LORI WAS GLAD SHE HAD ARRIVED at the Fall Festival early. It gave her time to get hold of herself and become accustomed to the bright lights in the auditorium, to the hustle and bustle, the atmosphere of expectancy.

She was grateful that her dad had sensed her need to be able to sit there quietly and had volunteered to bring her early. He gave her a parting pat on the shoulder and said, "I'm voting for you whether you win first prize or not," then moved to the center to reserve seats for the others.

Lori sat a few rows back, over to the left. That way she could sit sideways in her seat and observe the crowd without being obvious.

Old Mr. Jeffrey was two rows behind. He looked unnatural and uncomfortable in his Sunday-go-to-meetin' suit, as he called it. But he had come, and that was important to Lori.

As the auditorium filled, she spotted Mike sitting with Randy and that talkative little Karen. Did she have a crush on Randy? Imagine! Kids that age starting to notice the opposite sex. If they only knew! It wasn't all perfume and roses. There was a lot of agony involved in falling in love. Lori knew.

Ah! Darlene came through the entry, wearing a red velvet dress. She would! There was no denying it. Red was "her" color with that shiny blond hair and light skin.

If only Lori's hands weren't wet with perspiration. Already her hanky was a wadded gray ball. And the festivities hadn't even started yet. Her eyes darted from face to face. Had Ken come and she missed him? There he was now, coming in with Gibson, Dave, Shorty and Joe. Debby, Joan and Pam were giggling in a huddle behind, sort of waiting, Lori guessed, to see where the boys would sit so they could maneuver to sit beside or behind them.

The noise of the tuning of the violins and flutes grated on Lori. If only the orchestra could play their precious music without all that squawking! Of course the choir would sing.

158

Lori fidgeted. Do they have to have all those kids sing to make sure a crowd comes? What a bore!

Seats were rapidly taken. Lori turned around far enough to be able to glance at the clock below the balcony. The opening moment was close! Her heart thumped wildly, her hands were stiff from cold and dampness, her face hot and flushed.

Why did she ever think she could draw? Why hadn't she been content with squiggles on her notebook or caricatures for the neighbor kids?

Time, now, to sit around facing the front. The conductor's baton paused in mid-air. Ah, real music! Stirring music. Fitting music for the beginning of a really great evening. The festival was under way!

The music was pleasant to listen to, really. But it went on and on. The choir sang between times to give the members of the orchestra a rest, Lori supposed.

Finally, the school principal got up and cleared his throat. "Folks," he began, "the climax to this spectacular Fall Festival is the announcement of the winners in our contest. It was a contest conceived to discover the talented person who should have the honor of painting the mural in our fine new library . . ."

On and on. Why doesn't he come to the point?

wondered Lori. Yes, we know. There were many fine sketches entered. Sure. The judges had a rough time. Judges always do. *Three* prizes? Oh. There'll be two smaller murals for the runners-up to paint. And two lesser prizes. The poor judges really did have a bad time. Well, out with it! Who won the first prize. . . ? Honorable mentions, too? Three of them. You'll begin with them and work back to first prize. Sure. Keep us in suspense. You're doing a good job.

Quickly, Lori did a few mental gymnastics. She didn't want to hear her name called until five names had been told first. None of the three honorable mentions were acceptable to her. She didn't even want third or second prize. It was first prize she was after.

Suddenly, the hush of expectancy settled over the crowd.

"Jed Clark! Honorable mention!" Mild applause. "Marjorie McDaniel! Honorable mention!" More mild applause. "Dave Sawyer! Honorable mention!" More polite applauding.

Lori inched to the edge of her chair. Was she one of the real prize winners?

"Sandy Ryan! Stand up, Sandy."

Clapping was spontaneous.

"Don't hurry away, folks, after the conclusion of the program. The winning entries will be unveiled in the lounge. The proud winners will be there to accept your congratulations. The good ladies of the community have prepared refreshments. Smell the coffee? Ha, ha, ha."

Don't try so hard to be funny! Who's the winner? Who?

A glance in Darlene's direction revealed her to be poised — in a tense sort of way — but still poised.

Again, the principal was looking at his paper to fix in his mind the name of the winner of the second prize. Why were educators always nearsighted? Or was it his middle age showing? Deliberately, dramatically, he removed his glasses, enjoying the suspense he sensed from the crowd.

"Lori Goodman! As I said before, folks, it was a difficult choice. Most difficult. But second prize goes to a sophomore, Miss Lori Goodman. Stand up, Lori! Give her a hand, folks!"

Applause was enthusiastic and there were even a few whistles to liven things up.

Lori stood and managed a smile. Second prize was great. But it wasn't first! Was that pounding in her ears the sound of pounding hooves? Were they getting further away?

Once more there was a great forced silence. The name of the first-prize winner was about to be announced. Lori dropped to her seat. She knew who it was even before the principal said it.

"Darlene Pruitt! Our winner! Give her a big

hand, folks. Now, if the two young ladies, yes, all three — where's Sandy Ryan? If you three will come forward, I'll award the cash prizes."

Radiant in her red velvet dress, Darlene led the way to the platform. Lori fell in behind her and Sandy came last. Lori tried to sort out her thoughts. A cash prize for each of them? So intent had she been on getting first prize, she had almost forgotten that there was a second prize of one hundred dollars and a third prize of fifty.

Second prize! It was quite an honor, really. But the joy of being among the top three was dwarfed by the overwhelming realization that Darlene, of all people, was considered to be better than she! It was true, actually. Darlene could draw. It was just that Lori hated to admit it.

Now the principal handed out the prize envelopes, still talking about how hard it had been for the judges to make up their minds.

A mumbled, "Thanks," was all Lori said as she accepted the prize.

It was all over.

Again the orchestra played something loud with a good beat. Folks gathered around the platform to congratulate the winners while the principal tried to herd the three girls out a side door and around to the lounge. He wanted them beside their sketches for the proper background as well-wishers surged forward.

Darlene and Lori eased through a door at the same time.

Lori murmured, "Congratulations, Darlene. It's nice you won first prize."

It was the right thing to say. Lori hoped it didn't sound as forced as it really was.

"Why, thank you, Lori," Darlene gushed. "I'm dying to see your sketch. You've kept it such a secret. I hoped I'd see it Halloween night, but you didn't let me peek, did you? Randy sure talked a lot about it, though. I'll bet he even thinks you should have won first prize instead of his own sister! He might just be right, too."

Lori shook her head. "Of course not," she mumbled.

"Well, congratulations to you, anyway, on receiving second prize. It's really an honor!"

Lori managed an unenthusiastic "Thanks." She was glad her tears of disappointment couldn't be seen in the darkened hallway. By the time they reached the lounge, she had hold of herself.

As Lori stood there by her sketch, now unveiled, and she felt the warmth and sincerity of those who came to congratulate her, the importance of having a prize at all surged over her.

Gradually, Lori began to revel in the fact that she was second-prize winner with one hundred dollars in an envelope now tucked safely in her father's pocket. For the moment, thoughts of jealousy and disappointment at not winning first prize were subdued. Her father's warm, "I'm proud of you, Lori," had made her radiant.

Dad's as proud of me as though I'd won first prize instead of second, Lori thought. That's nice. Good old Dad! A comfortable feeling settled over her.

Before the next person came, Lori had time to glance beyond Darlene. With practiced eye, Lori took in the details of the prize-winning entry.

I guess it's no lie that the judges had a hard time, flashed through her mind. Darlene's drawing *is* good. Why am I so jealous? Why not accept the fact that the one who drew that picture is talented — even if it is Darlene?

Yielding to a charitable attitude relaxed Lori. She turned back to accept more congratulations.

Who was next? It was Mom and Mike who'd come to smile and beam and kiss and squeeze.

They moved on to make room for others.

Old Mr. Jeffrey shuffled toward Lori, his watery blue eyes shining with pride and contentment. He was thinking, no doubt, not only of Lori's talent, but of the honored place the old homestead log cabin would have in the attempt of the local folks to preserve some of the history of their town for coming posterity. To think that little Olaf would stand there pumping water for

164

his ma long after both were in their graves! For no amount of rationalizing could convince the old man that the boy was Mike Goodman. To him, it was himself as he had been so many decades before, little barefooted Olaf. The squeeze he gave Lori's hand was more eloquent than words.

Yes, Lori learned, there would be not one mural, but three. When the judges had such a difficult time deciding, they approached the committee with the suggestion that the allotted space be divided so that three panels would commemorate the courage of the early pioneers instead of only one. That meant that Darlene's picture would be in the center, but only slightly larger than Lori's or Sandy's. Lori cringed a little at the prospect of having to enlarge the sketch so much. Why, Storm would be almost life-size on the finished picture. Well, not quite, but almost.

Sometime at the height of the activity there in the lounge, Lori's father reached his left hand across through the crowd to offer her a paper cup of punch. Lori accepted it gratefully. The inside of her mouth was dry and she was licking her lips, vainly trying to moisten them.

Now the crowd thinned. Toward the back, against the wall, stood Ken! Was he purposefully waiting until there was more time to linger? To whom would he go first, to Darlene, or to her? She tried to appear nonchalant.

Then he was right there beside Lori, squeezing both her hands!

"Great! Just great!" He was smiling down at her. His voice went low and he bent close so only Lori could catch his next words. "Stupid judges! They made a mistake!"

Lori's heart flip-flopped. She flashed a radiant smile at Ken, happy that he would have cast the final vote in her favor. That took most of the sting of the disappointment that had been hers at coming in second to Darlene. Ken's vote of approval was worth more than that of the real judges.

Lori wore a smile that would not wipe off.

Before moving on to speak to Darlene, Ken paused to say, "Something exciting has happened!" His voice was so low Lori had trouble catching the words. But the sparkle in his eyes told her that it mattered very much to him.

"What?"

"Wait! I'll tell you at Darlene's party. You're coming, aren't you?"

Lori shrugged.

"Sure you are. She said the party would be for celebrating and you're one of the winners, aren't you?" He lowered his voice even more. "The prettiest one."

Lori turned her head, giggling, to hide her embarrassment.

Randy chased Mike down the hall. He skidded to a stop in front of Lori.

"Don't tell Sis," he said, glancing her way, "but those judges need to have their eyes examined. I'm not kidding! Who likes a train being loaded with logs better than a log cabin with a boy pumping water and a neat horse looking over his shoulder? Even if the sawmill is in front of some awfully pretty mountains with the leaves turning red and yellow. They goofed!"

Lori enjoyed Randy's candor. But she shushed him by saying, "It's all right, Randy. With Sandy's picture of main street in the good ol' days it will be a set of pictures that gives the feeling of the way life was way back when. Don't say anything to hurt Darlene," Lori added with a charitable surge.

Now, Lori remembered that Ken's comment had made her feel good all over. And he had exciting news he was going to share.

What could it be?

14

A New Look at Darlene

As soon as her father brought the car to a halt in the circular driveway, Darlene jumped out.

"Follow me, gang," she called above the chatter and door banging. "I want you to see the surprise Dad brought me last time he came home from a trip. Then I'll show you the new studio."

It was Ken who had made sure that he rode in the same car as Lori. Were her days of maneuvering over? He was right behind her, now, as the group trooped into the rambling, modern ranch house.

Darlene bounded ahead of the others, but she stopped by the couch in the large family room. "Guess what, Mummy!" she said. "I won! First prize. Can you believe it?"

While Darlene talked, the woman, reclining on one elbow, reached over the side of the couch, searching with one hand for something. She grasped an object, moved it behind a potted rubber plant, then, pretending to have been listening all along, gave Darlene her full attention.

"Good for you, Honey. Sorry I couldn't be there. This headache has me flat out." She rubbed her forehead with the back of one hand. "Poke the fire, will you, please? Marie's made refreshments. Tell her when you're ready."

Darlene nodded to Joe to go ahead and stir the fire, while she moved over to a large cage in the corner.

"Come here, Perky. You have company." Darlene opened the cage door and took out a young monkey, who clasped a long arm around Darlene's neck. The monkey, excited by strangers, screeched noisily.

While everyone else was exclaiming over the unusual pet, Lori's eyes were straining to see what Mrs. Pruitt had tried to conceal. Sure enough. There behind the potted plant was a bottle, a brandy bottle. Lori began to understand. There was a reason for that headache!

Soon Darlene was leading her guests through the breezeway, up the steps covered with indoor-outdoor carpeting, to her studio. Indirect lighting from the ceiling created a warm glow. Trays of open-face sandwiches, and plates of cakes and cookies, and pitchers of punch looked tempting.

"It's beautiful," Ken whispered to Lori. "But your loft has . . . atmosphere!" She gave Ken a grateful glance.

Now Darlene's dad stood at the door, a woman about his age beside him.

"Come in, Dad. Hi, Aunt Frieda. Hey, everybody. I want you to meet my aunt, Mrs. Walford. Aunty, I'll tell you everybody's name, although I don't suppose you'll remember . . ." and she proceeded to name her guests. "Aunty's here from New York. Came in time for Thanksgiving and the Fall Festival. Isn't that nice? Now help yourselves to the goodies. Marie can bring more."

All the time Lori was selecting from the array of attractive sandwiches, she had the feeling that Darlene's aunt was eyeing her. A glance in the woman's direction proved that she was right. Embarrassed, Lori looked away. She couldn't wait to get Ken into a secluded corner so she could hear the great news that had put a light into his eyes.

But before she could steer the conversation to Ken's promise, Mrs. Walford pulled a chair up and waited for a lull in their conversation.

Lori had noticed her at the festival, and had

171

wondered who she was. No one in their town wore her hair piled up in a mass of perfect curls. The home folks didn't go in for long dangling earrings, either. The air of sophistication stamped the newcomer as being "big-city," and Lori resented her intrusion into the privacy she was trying to create in the crowd.

"I remember your name," Mrs. Walford said. "You're Lori. And although I went through the line of well-wishers in the lounge, I want to say again that I think your talent is exceptional, my dear."

Between bites of olives and salted nuts, Lori smiled politely. "Thank you. I'm glad you like my work, Mrs. Walford."

"It's lovely, really, that Darlene placed high in the contest," Mrs. Walford said. Then her mood changed and in a low voice she added, "Poor dear! I feel sorry for her!"

Sorry for Darlene? That was a new one. Never had Lori felt sorry for Darlene, of all girls!

Lori recalled the appearance of the inside of the house. It was so rich looking, so just right. And who else's dad had money for a monkey? They didn't cost just peanuts. Who else's dad would have been quick to pull out his checkbook to pay for anything his daughter's heart desired?

Crowding into her mind's eye was the picture of a bejeweled hand searching for a brandy bottle to move behind the rubber plant.

Could Darlene's mother have a drinking problem? She had seemed to want to hide that bottle without anyone's noticing. Perhaps the aunt was right! If this were true, no wonder the remark, "Poor dear! I feel sorry for her!"

Lori took a bite of a cream cheese sandwich and glanced at Ken. He was listening to Mrs. Walford tell about some of the funny things that happened to her as an editor in the East.

Feigning polite interest, Lori withdrew mentally, intent upon the discovery she felt she had just made. She was beginning to see what made Darlene tick.

Lori felt ashamed. If what she was thinking was true, her continued resentment toward Darlene was unjustified. Was part of it based on rivalry over Ken's attention? Perhaps. But no matter what was behind it, it wasn't good. She knew that. No one had to tell her.

Suddenly, Lori realized that she hated Darlene mostly for what she privately called Darlene's "stuck-up-ishness." It was her easy possession of things, expensive things, that got Lori. It seemed as though in the Goodman household they always had to be scrimping and saving and cutting corners where money was concerned, now, especially since her dad's accident. But even in their financial crisis, Lori could always bank on her mom and dad's love. Actually, it was God's love reflected in the things her parents said and did, the way they looked at her. Sometimes, in fact, she almost felt smothered by that love. No, it wasn't smothering. It was a wonderfully secure feeling.

Lori glanced around at the hanging lamps, the built-in bookcase, the easel, the stool here in Darlene's studio. Everything was perfect — too perfect. It had taken money, lots of it. Had Darlene's dad put any of himself into the project? Foolish question!

Lori felt the crimson creep into her cheeks. Her own dad had spent hours turning her loft from a dream into a reality. It was slow work, handicapped as he was, but he did it because of his love for her. Lori was confident of that.

Again, a vision of that bottle shoved so slyly behind the rubber plant flashed into Lori's mind.

Her own mom complained sometimes, but that was because she was tired. It wasn't a bitter complaining—just a "I-wish-I-could-do-all-that's-expected-of-me" complaint. Lori's helping more would improve that situation. But that her mother loved her very much, Lori never doubted. That her mother loved the Lord and wanted God's best, always, for her daughter was a known fact. Even her not wanting Lori to have another horse was a proof of her love. From her mother's viewpoint, it was a way of protecting someone who was dear to her. Mom just didn't understand about horses.

While she and Mike had verbal scuffles, they loved each other underneath. Yes, love in her home could be spelled with a capital L. That was the one ingredient that seemed to be missing in Darlene's home.

Somewhere in her subconscious, she was struggling with an idea that insisted on surfacing. Darlene needed her for a friend! What she didn't need was silent resentment and sometimes open hostility.

She knew her attitude toward Darlene had become an ugly habit, one it wouldn't be easy to break. The writer of Ephesians in her Living Bible put it so plainly, there was no room for argument. It said, "Stop being mean, bad-tempered and angry. Quarreling, harsh words and dislike of others should have no place in your lives. . . ."

When she read that she was tempted to slam the Bible shut. Its words made her feel guilty, guilty about the mean, bad-tempered, shoddy way she treated Darlene day after day. *Harsh words and dislike of others have no place in your lives.* Okay, Lord, okay! You win. You're right. But tell me how I'm going to change. Just tell me that!

Only that day, her eyes had sought out the next few lines: "Instead, be kind to each other, tenderhearted, forgiving one another, just as God has forgiven you because you belong to Christ."

She knew she couldn't simply pray that God would do all the changing that needed to be done in her heart. No. She could depend on God to *help* her with her problem. He'd promised. But she was going to have to put some effort into effecting the desired change. Was she willing?

Pushing these thoughts from her mind, Lori focused her attention on Darlene's aunt.

"Just before I came West, I accepted a book about horses," Mrs. Walford said, glancing at Lori. "I think teenagers will enjoy it."

Lori murmured something about loving horses, and that she would like to read the book when it was published.

When the party came to an end, Lori realized that there hadn't been a moment when Ken could have shared his good news. As they came down the steps from the studio, he leaned over and whispered, "You want to go with me Sunday to measure the stream? In the afternoon. I'll tell you then."

Lori nodded. "Sure. Call me tomorrow."

Lori was the first to be delivered home by Darlene's dad. She called a quick "Thank you. It was a great party," and was soon in her own living room.

Her dad sat there, reading. In answer to Lori's questioning glance, he nodded toward the bedroom. "She's tired, these days. I doubt if she's asleep, yet, though. Why don't you see?"

Lori knocked gently on the bedroom door, then opened it in answer to her mother's call. The two talked about the festival and Lori's having won second prize. She told her mom about the party, the monkey, the lovely studio, the tasty refreshments and Darlene's interesting aunt. She said nothing about Mrs. Walford's concern for her niece.

Giving her mother a kiss on the cheek, Lori closed the bedroom door and stood beside her father. She realized that lately she and her dad hadn't had any of the private conversations that were important to them both.

"I was real proud of you," her dad said in his soft voice.

Lori smiled and kissed her dad on the forehead. She dropped to the stool at his feet, and sat, chin in her hands, elbows resting on her knees.

She knew her father was studying her face, trying to figure out what she was thinking. He would wait patiently, until she was ready to share what seemed to be troubling her.

Finally, Lori blurted, "Dad, is there anybody you just can't stand?"

"Well, now, there have been some at different times in my life, Lori. But I found a long time ago that the person I hated wasn't hurt much by what was churning inside of me. I was hurt. The jealousy and resentment and hatred inside were shriveling my soul, or whatever you want to call the real you that is inside you." He poked at the fire, musing. "Of course, I still run across people who tend to irk me. But I've learned to be understanding. I think, 'What makes this person tick? Why is he the way he is? How would I act if I were in his shoes? And can there be anything I can do to help this person be different? Maybe he has a problem and hates himself for the way he is.'"

Mr. Goodman glanced sideways at his daughter. "On the other hand, Lori, when I'm irked by somebody, more than likely it's *me* that needs changing. The other person may be acting the only way he can under the circumstances and it's *my* attitude that needs to be pulled out and examined."

Lori nodded. "I've been resentful for an awfully long time." She paused, her eyes following the flickering flames. "I'm beginning to see that it's not the other person who needs changing. It's me." Sensing the question mark on her father's face, she went on. "That is, this other person has a problem, one I never dreamed existed. I'm still not sure about it, but I'm beginning to wonder. . . ."

Flames licked at the logs, popping, glowing, dancing.

"While I can't solve this person's . . . oh, you might as well know! It's Darlene! I can't solve her great enormous problem. Still, maybe there's something I can do to make her happier." She picked up the poker her dad had laid on the hearth and idly rearranged the half-burned logs. "I mean, she doesn't seem unhappy. But she is, really. She can't help being with a mother who . . . well, who must have a big problem and a dad who. . . ."

Lori sat silent, hugging her knees, thinking. Her dad didn't pry. Instead, he slipped an arm around her and gave her a hug. He knew she would share with him all that she wished to share.

Abruptly, Lori jumped to her feet. "It's been a long day. We're both tired."

Her dad stood, too. "I'm proud of you, Lori," he said softly. "Your mother and I both are. Now get some sleep."

Moments later, Lori snuggled beneath the blankets.

Certain thoughts chased themselves in her mind. "Darlene is insecure. Darlene craves attention and love. Darlene is a good actress. Most

179

of all, Darlene needs to know how very much God loves her. . . ."

She winced in the darkness. It was easy to sing piously in church week after week about loving, serving, helping others. Was she prepared to *live* the things she sang?

Here was a challenge. . . .

Was she able . . . was she *willing* to meet it?

15

Storm Steps Out

Lori was disappointed that she would have to wait until Sunday afternoon before Ken could share his good news, but Saturday promised to be eventful. This was the day Mr. Granberg had said she could ride Storm for the first time. He would be there to instruct and to assist, of course.

Remembering how Storm bucked that first time he mounted sent shivers through Lori. She had seen Mr. Granberg ride her, the last few days, under perfect control, or so it seemed. But no horse is completely predictable. Mr. Granberg was an experienced rider and horse-trainer. If Storm sensed that Lori was fearful, how would the horse react? Would Lori be able to communicate the fact that she was in control and must be obeyed? Lori was apprehensive, yet thrilled.

When Lori's mother said that she and Mike were going to town to begin Christmas shopping and that Lori could go if she wanted, Lori quickly said she preferred to wait.

"I'll have dinner started so it will be easy to put on when you get back," Lori said, relaxing when her mother seemed pleased at her having volunteered this help.

After the car pulled out of the driveway, Lori stirred up a jello fruit salad. That way, if her mother had forgotten something, she wouldn't discover her daughter heading down the Old Burn Road. When she was sure that her mother and Mike were on their way, she found her bike and was off.

She'd forgotten about her dad. He'd mentioned that he had a cord of wood to stack down by the front fence. She could have detoured through the woods if she had remembered. Now, of course, he wanted to know where she was off to.

"Mr. Granberg is training Storm," she blurted. "I love to watch. He doesn't care a bit. I'll be back in time to start dinner like I promised Mom. The salad is done already."

Lori's father paused, leaning on a cedar fence post. "Any chance of that Bronson boy being

182

there to watch the bronco busting too?" His eyes twinkled.

Lori blushed. Then, wanting to change the subject, she said, "Dad, you promised I could have another horse . . . sometime. When do you think that 'sometime' will be?"

The twinkle faded from her father's eyes.

"I wish I could tell you, Lori. I know a horse is important to your happiness." He sighed. "We can't afford it right now. You know that. Even if we could, your mother has to be won over." He glanced at his right arm. "I don't know what it would take to make her willing to have another horse here at Marycrest."

"She's partly right, I suppose," Lori conceded. "There are accidents with horses. Still, people fall down in their kitchens. They have automobile accidents, too, and . . . all kinds of things. We have to just go on living, enjoying what we can."

Lori's eyes searched her father's face. "You won't be living — *really* living, until you have a horse to ride again, Dad. You know that!"

"You and I know it, Lori, even if your mother doesn't," he said reluctantly.

Lori shrugged and turned to go.

That settled it!

If Lori could manage to bring a well-trained Storm onto the place through her own efforts so the family would not be faced with one more financial obligation, her dad would welcome the mare.

Her mother? Well, that was a problem she'd have to think about some other time. Right now, mounting Storm and staying on her was the business at hand.

Lori found Storm pacing back and forth in the yard adjoining the stall area. When Lori called, the mare pricked her ears forward, then quickly came to the sound of the familiar voice. Unhesitatingly, she "shook hands" before Lori gave her the usual apple.

Mr. Granberg was now at Lori's elbow. "Go ahead and saddle and bridle her, Lori. This is your day. Let's see how well you two get along. If all goes well, before too long I want to get her back to Bronson. Got other horses coming in and I need the stall."

Snapping a lead rope to the halter, Lori tied Storm to the rail fence near the tackroom door and began to groom.

"Take your time," called Mr. Granberg. "I'll be working this gelding until you're ready."

Lori had already tied on the carpenter's apron after feeling in the big pockets to make sure all the brushes and tools she would need were there. Body brush, dandy brush, currycomb, finishing cloth. Mane and tail comb and hoof-pick.

"Ready, old girl?" Lori said.

Taking the rubber currycomb in her right hand and the body brush in her left, Lori started to clean the mare's left side, using circular motions. Lori was an experienced groomer; she didn't just dab at the horse, but leaned with her weight as she worked. Feet, mane, tail, all were attended to. And last of all, a quick going-over with the finishing cloth, left the mare shining and sleek.

"I'll bet you're not just part-Arabian, Storm. Mr. Bronson says we have to call you a part-Arab because we can't prove you're purebred. I wonder if that old man who gave you to the boys' school had papers for you?"

As Lori worked, her mind raced. Why not write to the boys' school? She'd ask for the name of the donor, then write the man a letter, asking if the mare had been registered. If she had been,

Storm would really be a valuable horse. Lori didn't want the price to be raised so she'd have no chance of buying the horse. Yet, she felt she must know, if possible, if the mare was registered.

"I love you, Storm," she said, "whether you're purebred Arabian or not. Still, it would be nice to know."

When Storm was groomed, saddled and bridled, Lori led her to the arena, carefully sliding the gate shut.

The moment of truth had arrived!

Mr. Granberg was inside the arena, now, too. "You're in command, Lori. Feel it. Then the mare'll feel it, too."

Lori gathered up the reins and stood, prepared to mount. She held a whip in her left hand. Remembering, she allowed Storm to sniff it, to explore it with her soft, rubbery lips.

"I won't use it on you, Storm, if you behave. I hope that your just seeing it will remind you that I'm in charge. Ready, old girl?"

Again, Lori gathered up the reins, her left hand on Storm's withers.

Where was all of Lori's courage?

Now! Left foot into the stirrup. Stand erect, pause, right leg over. Slowly. Settle down into the saddle. Hold the reins loosely, but firmly.

"Prancing a bit, old girl, aren't you? Steady. That's a good Storm."

Leaning forward, Lori patted the sleek skin affectionately.

"Nice going." Mr. Granberg grinned.

Slowly, deliberately, Lori began to push the mare's sides with her legs. This was the signal that told the mare to walk forward. Amazingly, without any funny business, Storm stepped out. Because Storm had obeyed, Lori let up the leg pressure.

Around the arena they went. With each step Storm took, Lori relaxed a bit more. But she didn't relax her grip on the reins. That was the mistake her father had made.

After a while, Lori pulled on the reins, giving little squeezes, saying, "Whoa," as she did so. Storm stopped and Lori let the reins hang loose. It was the signal Storm was apparently waiting for. She stood still.

Again, Lori leaned forward and patted Storm's neck. "Good girl," she said. "Good old Storm!"

Mr. Granberg never took his eyes off Storm and Lori for the half hour Lori rode.

"That's enough for today," he called. "We don't want to tire her."

There was no problem in getting off. Lori led Storm around the arena a couple of times. She hadn't worked the mare enough to sweat her up, but Storm was wet with perspiration from nervous exhaustion. Walking would cool her, and a good rubdown with a clean sack was in order.

This done, Storm was turned loose. She trotted away, then rolled in the dirt.

"Come back Monday," Mr. Granberg called to Lori. "If all goes well, you should be able to ride her up to Bronsons'. I'll take her on the road tomorrow to see how she reacts to cars. She learns fast, that mare. Smart as they come. You sure she isn't a purebred Arabian? Anybody got papers on her?"

"Not that we know of," Lori answered. Under her breath she added, "but I aim to find out . . . on my own!"

Back home, Lori put a cake into the oven, then glanced at the clock and decided she had time to get a letter into the mailbox before the mailman came. There wasn't much to say. Just that she wanted to know the name of the man who had made a present of the mare to the boys' school, and his address. She enclosed a self-addressed, stamped envelope. Maybe nothing would come of the query. Anyway, she would try.

After grabbing a sandwich, Lori wondered how to spend the afternoon hours before it was time to start dinner. Should she go to Darlene's? She hadn't done that since they were in pigtails. Since they'd grown up, they had been rivals, not friends. But underneath Darlene's seeming poise was a lonely, unloved, frightened girl. Darlene's aunt had said so. And she seemed to be a person who knew what she was talking about.

Besides, it would stand to reason that if your mother had a drinking problem and your dad was always away on business, you'd feel lonely. Just having a roof over your head and plenty of food and even plenty of really nice things, even things most kids never dreamed of having, didn't guarantee happiness.

Lori knew this must be an old truth, but it was as though she had just discovered it. Instead of finding jealousy in her heart when she thought of Darlene, she felt sympathy. The feeling nagged at Lori to do something about it.

Lori wasn't quite sure just what she should do. If whatever she decided were too obvious, Darlene would become suspicious. Who wants obvious sympathy?

No, Lori would have to be subtle.

Finally, she decided to call the Pruitt residence and ask for Mrs. Walford. She'd confided in Lori and Ken at the party. They were friends, now, sort of. Perhaps she would like to see Lori's Loft. Yes, that was a good angle. Mrs. Walford seemed to appreciate Lori's art. The aunt might like to see where she worked.

Lori would ask the woman to bring her niece along. That would be a good way. Darlene might suspect that the invitation was only a polite "must" because of the aunt's coming, but Lori would be so warm and kind toward her classmate that she would soon see Lori's true motive of wanting to be a friend.

Lori was proud of her new charitable feelings. She had made a start in breaking that old "hate" habit. So far, so good!

She made the call and it was arranged. She could hear muffled arguing in the background when Mrs. Walford turned to tell Darlene that she was included in the invitation. But the word that came back through the receiver was, "We'll come. Both of us!"

Lori hurried to stir up icing for the cake so she'd have something to serve.

Suddenly, she remembered what Darlene had said to Ken that day on the school bus. "I'm horse hunting, did you know? I hear Mr. Granberg is doing a great job in breaking Storm. That horse has sure got the class and looks I'm after. . . . It won't matter what the price is. . . ."

Lori stirred the icing madly. "I'll be a friend to you, Darlene Pruitt," she hissed, "but just keep your hands off Storm. She's all mine. Or she *will* be someday. I hope!"

Hearing the doorbell, Lori wiped her hands on her apron, tried to toss out ugly thoughts, and put on her best smile for her guests.

16

Not the Only Horse
in the World

MRS. WALFORD'S ADMIRATION of Lori's Loft was profuse and sincere. "The old schoolhouse clock with its swinging pendulum, the potbellied stove, the round-topped trunk—why, you've some priceless antiques here, my dear," she told Lori. "Even the rough-looking barn walls you've left for two sides make your loft right up to date. Weathered wood is used in modern homes. Did you know that?"

Lori forced a smile. "Yes, I know," she said. A vision of flames dancing skyward on a chilly Halloween night flashed before her eyes. Then Lori opened the lid of the old trunk to pull out samples of her past work.

Mrs. Walford gushed on and on. "I like your

studio, Darlene. Believe me. But this Loft, as Lori calls her studio, has a flavor and character all its own. Don't you agree?"

Darlene's face clouded with a hurt expression Lori had never seen before. "It's because Lori's dad helped her dream it up. He went to the auction to get the old door, the stove, the clock. And he carved her nameplate with his one good hand. He did it even after the accident he had."

Darlene turned to look out the window. Was it so the other two wouldn't detect the tears welling up into her blue eyes?

"I wish my dad would care about me. Oh, sure. He's handy at writing checks. Big deal!"

Darlene shot a defiant glance in Lori's direction.

"In fact, the latest wrinkle is . . . you'd never guess. I have my *own* checking account, complete with personalized checks!"

Lori's jaw dropped in surprise.

Darlene hadn't finished. "Of course Dad put money in the account, quite a bit I'd say." She looked around the room. "I'd rather have my dad *show his love* like your dad does, Lori. It's . . . it's more convincing than money, even gobs of money."

Wide-eyed, Lori sat on a footstool, a pile of her drawings on her lap, pondering the emotions she sensed flowing through this girl whom she had always envied. Laying the drawings on the braided rug, Lori rose and went to Darlene's side. Standing close, she slipped an arm around her.

"I'm sorry," Lori said. She didn't want to come right out and say, "I'm sorry your dad doesn't talk much with you or do things with you. I'm sorry your mother is more interested in the brandy bottle than in anything else."

So Lori just stood there, hoping Darlene would understand that she, Lori, was groping, trying to find a way to show that she was sorry for the mean and spiteful way she'd been acting for so long, trying to show, by her close presence, that she sympathized and wanted to be a friend.

Mrs. Walford didn't seem to notice the little drama. "I see you have a chart describing the anatomy of the horse. Smart girl! No wonder your horse drawings come across so lifelike!"

Darlene swung around. "I really envy you, Lori. I've always wished I could draw horses like you do. Will you teach me how?"

Lori blushed. Darlene was a good artist. That she had won first prize in the contest was proof that others thought so. Yet she was asking Lori to teach her! Lori was flattered. She was also grateful. She recognized a natural way to show love and concern to this girl who had been doing a good job of concealing her true feelings.

"Sure. I'll show you what I know. I'll be

glad to! The first thing, I think, is to get a chart like this one I found in the paper." Lori moved close to the wall. "It was in the Sunday paper on October 26th. Do you think you can find it? When you know how the horse is put together, it's easier to make a lifelike animal."

"You used Storm for a model in your sketch, didn't you?" Darlene said. "I don't blame you for using her. She's really magnificent!"

Mrs. Walford's eyes scanned the bottles on the windowsill.

"Lori, child!" she exclaimed. "Where did you get those bottles?" She moved to the window and picked up a bottle to examine it. "Wouldn't the antique dealers back East go wild about these! A blue bottle, yet. And with a seam down the side and the little hollow on the bottom. That shows how very old the bottle is." She turned the bottle in her hand around and around. "It was made before the modern method of pouring and molding bottles was invented. Look! The top of this bottle tells that it's old, too. It's not a screw-on top. If it were, it would be worth less. How clever of you, Lori, to recognize the value of these items and collect them."

"I didn't know they were worth anything," Lori admitted. "I just thought they were pretty, that's all. I like the way the sunlight shines through the blue glass. That's why I decided to put them on the windowsill. They're just old bottles. Are they really valuable?"

"Oh, yes. How valuable I couldn't say. I'm not that well informed. But hang onto them!"

"I've always meant to go dig for more where I found those. The junk pile's become covered with leaves and moss over the years. But I've been so busy. . . ."

Darlene had been studying the chart of the horse and had not entered into the conversation about bottles. Now, she whirled to face Lori.

"I saw you riding Storm this morning," she said. "She was behaving like a perfect lady. You probably didn't see us. Aunt Frieda and I were returning from town so we stopped and watched you go around and around the arena. Storm stopped when you told her to and she went where you told her to. Mr. Granberg has done wonders with her. Of course, you had done a good job making friends, before that."

"Teaching her to shake hands was a big help in communicating," Lori said. She was beginning to feel uneasy. She liked to hear praise for her ability in gentling a horse and she loved to hear others admire Storm. But coming from Darlene and knowing what she had said about the horse to Ken, what did she mean? Darlene didn't keep her wondering.

"I've made up my mind I'm riding in the

Pioneer Days Parade. And I'm not riding Pokey! Since my dad put all that money in a checking account for me, I'm going to make Mr. Bronson an offer he'll have a hard time refusing!"

Lori stifled the impulse to protest loudly. Just when she had decided to be nice to Darlene, why did she have to trespass in the most important area of Lori's life?

You're sure making it hard for me to love you, Darlene Pruitt! Lori thought. She said, "True, Storm behaved well this morning. But no horse is completely dependable. I don't want to sound like I'm bragging. But it takes a pretty good horsewoman to show that mare who's in control. If you'd seen her buck when Mr. Granberg mounted her, you'd know what I mean. As he'd say, she's quite a bit of horse. Not just anyone could ride her."

Darlene's eyes flashed. "Are you insinuating that I don't know how to ride, Miss Know-it-all? If you can handle Storm, then I can, too. You'll see!"

"Girls, girls!" Darlene's aunt chided.

Chagrined, Lori moved to the window. She stood staring out, biting her lower lip.

Darlene picked up a pad and began to sketch the outline of the horse as pictured on the chart while her aunt watched, silent.

Darlene, now calm once more, asked Lori,

"What am I doing wrong?"

Lori whirled. The nerve of some people, she thought. She threatens to buy the very horse I have my heart set on. Then she asks my advice about art work. As if I cared!

Was it possible that Lori had felt sympathy for this arrogant girl? But she must not let Mrs. Walford be aware of her true feelings. Taking the sketch from Darlene's hand, she scanned it.

"Here," Lori said. She removed the tacks that held her article to the wall. "If you do the exercises pictured here, you'll get the feel for the proportions of the head. See. Make a long tapering cylinder. Divide the length into thirds. That shows where to put the eye. A line down . . . shows where the cheekbone comes. Get it?"

As Lori talked, she was busy with the pencil she had taken from Darlene's hand.

"You do it so easily!" Darlene exclaimed. "Thanks for lending me your article. I'll take good care of it and return it. I hope Marie hasn't thrown the old papers out yet. I need one of these to keep. Lori, you're great!"

Lori winced. She didn't feel great. Where were her good resolutions to be a true friend to Darlene? She'd made the impression, all right. What she felt deep inside was another thing. Now, like a broken record, words from her Living Bible said themselves over and over in Lori's head: Stop being mean, bad-tempered and angry. Stop being mean, bad-tempered and angry. Dislike of others should have no place in your lives. Dislike of others should have no place in your lives. Instead, be kind to each other, tenderhearted, forgiving one another. Instead, be kind . . .

Lori wanted to smash the broken record to bits. A better way would be to ask God to help her to be the person she knew He wanted her to be. But somehow, she wanted to clutch her ugliness a little longer. She couldn't tell why, but she did. Nobody would make her do otherwise, not even God.

Lori was grateful that her guests didn't know what she was thinking. The two left, presently, and Lori glanced at the clock. Time to start making meatballs for dinner. She was glad she returned to the kitchen when she did. The phone rang and it was Ken.

"I'll stop by for you to go measure the stream a little after three tomorrow. All set?"

"Fine! I'll hurry with dinner dishes. I'm sure I'll be free to go by then. I should wear boots, you said?"

"Yeah. There are a couple of marshy places."

"Do I have to wait until tomorrow for you to share that bit of news you have to tell me?"

"No reason why I can't tell you now, but I

think I'll keep you guessing."

"You're mean!"

"Mean, am I? Have it your way. The news is exciting to me, but it might not be to you, Lori. I don't know how it's all going to turn out. I hope that what seems to be developing in my favor won't turn out to be something that hurts you. I wouldn't want that." He paused. "Yet I can't quite see a really satisfactory solution so you and I will both be happy about it."

"Oh, you talk in riddles!"

"Sorry about that!"

"You are not sorry or you wouldn't make me wait . . . oh, I hear a car. They're back. I better get to my cooking. 'Bye, now. I'll be ready at three."

What could he be talking about?

The next day, Lori sat by Ken in Sunday school, but she knew it was no use trying to pry his news flash from him there. She'd just have to wait until the afternoon excursion when they were alone.

She hurried the serving of dinner so she could have time to get the dishes done before Ken arrived.

Ken was right on time. "Have a scarf?" he asked. "It's over a mile and it's cool in the woods."

Lori's heart sang. Ken needed her. Of course,

anyone could be his helper on his weekly mission. His father had often gone with him. But this time, he wanted *her!* Her cheeks glowed with the thrill of it.

Not wanting to seem too curious, she avoided asking about the news he had promised. They walked along, sometimes noticing birds or squirrels. They flushed a grouse and listened to the whirr of its wings. A doe and her yearling stood staring in the path ahead, ears alert, before bounding off into the woods.

Finally, Ken stopped. "Guess what!" he said.

"What?"

"Rowdy is going to be for sale and Joe promised I had first chance at him!"

"Is that the news?"

"Yep."

"Oh, Ken. I'm happy for you! You always did like Rowdy. It really is neat the way he stands high on his hind feet when his rider says, 'Up, Rowdy!' That *is* good news! Why shouldn't I be glad?"

Ken hesitated. "Well, Dad owes me a horse. I've been working for him with that as my reward. He's sorry he bought a horse I don't really care for so he's willing to get me Rowdy. Trouble is, he needs the money he sunk into Storm to swing the deal."

Lori felt the blood drain from her face, then

flush it once more. "Why, if Storm is going to be for sale, that's good news for me, too!" she exclaimed. "I have the hundred dollars in prize money. Besides my caricature and strawberry money. No problem. I can just about pay for Storm so you'll have money to pay for Rowdy. But how come Joe changed his mind?"

"It was Joe's dad who changed Joe's mind. He's being transferred to Florida and he refuses to haul Rowdy clear across the States. Says Joe can buy another horse with the money he gets from Rowdy. He wants cash right now, too. They're not even waiting for the semester to end."

Lori liked the slurpy sound the water in the marsh was making as she pulled her boots up, then put them down.

"I never dreamed Storm would be mine so soon!" she said.

"That's the bad part, Lori. Joe was at Darlene's house when she and her aunt left your loft. As soon as she heard that Rowdy was for sale — for cash only, she had her aunt take her right over to see my dad."

Ken eyed Lori closely.

Lori felt the color drain from her cheeks, once more.

Ken opened his mouth, but no words came out. Lori sensed he didn't want to tell her what **he** felt he must.

At last Ken went on. "Darlene has her own checking account. Did you know that?"

Lori nodded. "She told me. Said her dad had put money into an account for her, quite a bit of money."

"It must have been quite a bit!" Ken exclaimed. "The amount Darlene offered Dad for a mare that isn't even registered as half-Arabian, let alone purebred, would floor you!"

Lori dreaded hearing what Ken was going to say next, yet she knew she must. "Well?"

"Dad hesitated — it wasn't the price he was balking at, for it was three times what he hoped to get — it was the fact that he had always thought of Storm as going to you, Lori. That's if and when he decided to give her up."

Ken pulled a branch from a willow and twirled it nervously between his fingers.

"After all," he continued, "Storm wouldn't be the horse she is without all the time and effort you've put into training her. Dad knows that. But since he hesitated, Darlene said, 'Isn't that enough money, Mr. Bronson? Well, would you part with her for more?' She named an even more fantastic sum.

" 'You're out of your mind!' my dad told her. 'I have no papers for this mare.'

" 'I don't care about that!' Darlene said. 'Dad

isn't good at anything but making money. The check I'd write would be good, Mr. Bronson.'"

Lori said nothing. The two walked on in silence. Finally, Ken said, "If you ask me, Darlene was being spiteful, spending her dad's money that way. But my father didn't doubt that a check that size would be good."

"The witch!" Lori hissed. She glanced at Ken, hoping he hadn't heard.

"And like Dad told me later," Ken went on, "he figured with that amount of money, he could pay cash for Rowdy, and buy a good riding horse for himself, now that he's decided he'd like to do some more riding. He could even buy a good horse to give you, Lori, for all your trouble. That way all three of us would have horses. No, all four. Darlene would be happy, Dad and I would be happy and you'd be properly paid for your work." There was concern in Ken's voice as his eyes searched Lori's. "How does all this sound?"

Overwhelmed, Lori was speechless. "I . . . I don't know," she faltered.

Darlene had meant it, hadn't she? She could see herself astride the beautiful horse with the conformation of an Arabian, the mare's light mane and tail streaming in the breeze, her own blond hair matching the tail of the horse. A striking sight, anyone would admit.

But Lori's world had collapsed.

During the rest of the expedition, Lori was very quiet. She did exactly what Ken told her to do and waited patiently while he made notations in the notebook he pulled from his pocket. By his considerate manner and unruffled voice, Lori sensed that Ken felt the turmoil in her heart.

She'd soon have a horse of her own, yes. And wasn't that what she wanted very much? She desperately wanted a horse, not only for her own pleasure, but to make life more satisfying to her dad. The accident had robbed him of something that was dear to him. Owning a horse could restore that.

So, what was the problem?

"It was a hard decision to make," Ken said softly. "Dad did some serious thinking before he accepted that check. Come on, Lori. Storm isn't the only horse in the world. You'll learn to love another one just as much!"

Now Lori's eyes filled with tears. Biting her lip, she shook her head. Then, finding it impossible to control herself, she hid her face in her hands and sobbed. Even the feel of Ken's strong arm around her waist in an attempt to comfort didn't erase the hurt.

Storm was leaving her life for always.

And whose life was she entering? Darlene's, of all people!

17

Good-Bye to a Dream

MR. GRANBERG FOUND THAT Storm shied when cars passed her on the road so he decided to keep her a couple more weeks, even though his schedule was full.

Lori didn't really care. Since Storm was now Darlene's horse, she had little reason to be concerned about Storm's progress as a riding horse on a road, a trail, or anywhere else. But Mr. Bronson asked her to ride the mare daily for at least a month after the trainer was finished.

"For the price I'm accepting for that horse, I want to be able to turn over a first-class job," he explained.

Lori was silent, her eyes on a rock which she kept kicking aimlessly.

"I didn't mean to hurt you, Lori," Mr. Bronson continued. "I wish you'd believe me when I say it. This way, Ken gets his horse, the one he likes, and you and I both can have pretty good riding horses. If you look at it right, it's a break, I'd say."

She was unconvinced. "If I ride Storm an hour every day for the next few weeks, is my part of the bargain over?" she asked. Her voice was flat and colorless.

"Sure. Sure. Then we'll go shopping for two fine horses, you and I. If you hear of one you're interested in, in the meantime, just let me know." Mr. Bronson laid an arm around her shoulder. "Don't take it so hard, Lori, please. It'll all turn out for the best!"

Ken was on Rowdy, who was prancing around the pasture. He brought his horse to a stop near where his father and Lori were standing.

"UP, Rowdy, UP!" commanded Ken. He leaned forward, brushing his face on the horse's neck to keep his balance as Rowdy's front feet left the ground, pawing the air wildly.

As the gelding's forefeet touched the ground again, Ken called, "He minds me as well as he did Joe! Hey, Lori. Next Sunday we can ride to the stream to take the testings. Hurry up and find the horse you want Dad to buy. Then we can ride together anytime we want!"

Was Ken chummy because he pitied her? Was he friendly to cover up his father's seeming rashness? Or was Ken beginning to appreciate her and really wanting to be with her? She wished she knew.

"Wait!" There was no enthusiasm in her voice. "I've agreed to ride Storm every day for awhile. I might as well start or she'll forget part of what the trainer taught her." Lori began to saddle up. "Any salmon down at the river yet? Show us the trail. Okay?"

They could have gone to the river most of the way on paved road. But why do that when there were shortcuts that were mere trails? Rowdy insisted on being first, always. Even when the trail was an old logging road and wide enough for the two to ride side by side, Rowdy had to step out and be a neck ahead.

"It's because he's a Tennessee Walker," Ken explained. "I'm glad Dad likes him. He doesn't eat all that much, either. An easy keeper, is the way they put it. But Rowdy sure likes to step out and walk fast. Look at him go!"

"You got your 'man's horse,' didn't you? I'm glad about that."

Ken quickly glanced at Lori. "Are you being sarcastic, Lori, or are you really glad I have Rowdy?"

"I'm glad," Lori said. "I really am, Ken." No need to add that the circumstances surrounding the transaction made her feel sick.

The two directed their horses to walk the gravel bar by the river until they came to the rapids. Ken slipped off Rowdy — he was riding bareback — and tied the reins to a willow tree. Lori decided she had better stay right with Storm so she wouldn't spook at anything. Ken didn't argue. He waded into the water until he was knee deep and pushed his way upstream. Lori knew Ken enjoyed watching the thrashing bodies of the nearly spent male salmon. The last act of each would be to fertilize the eggs of some female, now burrowing a resting place in the sand at the river bottom.

She heard Ken's exclamations as he discovered an exceptionally large fish. She held her nose as the stinking body of a long-dead male floated downstream. She stroked Storm, loving her and not wanting to love her, for the day of final parting would be all the harder. Better to steel her heart against the horse than to allow love to flow.

What a predicament! Just when the horse was well broken for riding and was capable of giving so much pleasure! How Dad would have loved to have ridden such a horse, Lori thought. Papers, or no papers. Purebred or just Arabian-like, she was a superb horse. Lori knew she'd never find another like her.

The realization depressed her.

Storm rubbed Lori's arm and shoulder and back affectionately, it seemed to Lori, with her soft muzzle.

"Are you asking me to scratch behind your ears?" Lori asked. "Storm, you don't know what I know. Just about Christmastime you're going to go live with another girl. In fact, you're already hers. She'll be nice to you, Storm, I know. She wanted you very much."

She was glad Ken couldn't see her tears of self-pity. By the time he returned, her eyes were dry again. She forced a laugh at his wet, squishy shoes and dripping pants legs.

"Who cares?" Ken laughed back. "It's all part of this business of seeing salmon during spawning season. I'm ready to go back. Are you?"

Lori gathered the reins, put her hand on the withers, and mounted. It was hard to believe that this was the horse who had been bucking her rider just a few weeks before.

"You learned your lessons fast and well, didn't you, old girl?" Lori whispered into Storm's ear, patting her on the neck.

It became almost a daily occasion, this trail riding with Ken. He hurried with his chores in the barn and when the days became so short there was no daylight left after chores, he asked to be allowed to ride right after school, then do the chores by the light in the barn.

Lori, too, was able to do her helping-at-home tasks a little later. Her father had discovered that she was riding Storm daily. Something Mike and Randy had said led him to do a little detective work on his own. When faced with a direct question, Lori readily admitted the part she had had in gentling Storm and told what was still required of her. She carefully omitted the details about Darlene's huge check and that she was to be given the riding horse of her choice in return for her services. Somehow, the thrill of knowing she would soon have a horse of her own was overshadowed at the thought of giving Storm up, and to Darlene, at that! Besides, she didn't want to risk hearing from her mother, "You know what I said! No more horses at Marycrest. The grief they've caused already!"

Lori knew her dad didn't agree. He was a horse-lover and he always would be. He wasn't going to blame a green-broke horse for his own oversight. A real horseman expects to be thrown a few times in a lifetime of horseback riding. He takes the consequences in stride. He doesn't get rid of the horses in his life. He just tries to anticipate awkward situations and avoid them. But Lori's mother was adamant. Her dad kept quiet, realizing his wife's attitude grew out of love and concern.

Because she was still working, Mom wasn't aware of Lori's being away so regularly day after day, so she hadn't asked questions.

Feeling badly that he would be unable to replace Bucky-B for a very long time, maybe never, Lori's father was glad that Lori was having this pleasure from Bronson's horse. He told her so.

"I would have been nervous had I known what was going on earlier," he confided, "but now that the mare has been handled by Mr. Granberg, I feel relaxed. There is no better trainer anywhere than Granberg. We would have been way ahead if we had given him Bucky-B to train."

Christmas, usually such a joyous time of year for Lori, became a date to dread. That's when Darlene would take delivery. That's when Lori and Storm would say good-bye forever.

So quiet and unresponsive was Lori concerning decorating the house and tree and baking little extras, that Lori's mother wondered if she were sick.

"I'm going to make an appointment with Dr. Vogan for early next week," she said. "It's time you had a thorough checkup."

"There's nothing wrong with me," Lori protested. "I'm OK."

But her mother made the appointment. There was very little the matter, however, just a slight iron deficiency which could easily be taken care of with a pill a day.

"She's in excellent health," the doctor said.

But that only baffled her mother. She felt sure something was wrong. When the doctor didn't discover what it was, she didn't know which way to turn and said so.

"I'm all right," Lori insisted. "Don't worry about me, Mom."

On Christmas Eve afternoon, Ken told Lori he'd have to forego the daily trail ride. "Mom has a lot of chores she wants me to do. I have to make sure there's plenty of wood handy for the fireplace. The house will be full of relatives for our Christmas Eve celebration tonight."

Lori was actually relieved.

Riding alone, she could take her last ride on Storm without having to seem carefree when her heart was aching. The horse knew the way to the stream Ken measured, then automatically took the trail down to the river. There was an open stretch on the logging road where they always let their horses race. Anticipating a good run, Storm quickened her walk as they approached the edge of the woods. Slight pressure from Lori's legs signaled the mare to gallop. Another bit of pressure told her she was to break into a run.

Lori gave Storm her head. The mare was at liberty to run as fast as she wished.

How she ran! Lori's black hair flew behind and her cheeks turned red from the biting December wind. She enjoyed every delicious moment, but at the same time she was overwhelmed with a dreadful heaviness.

Darkness was settling. Lori reined Storm for the return trip, signaling her to a walk. Soon it would be only a memory—the pleasure derived from Storm's smooth movement beneath.

Back at the Bronson barn, she cooled the mare, then brushed her and rubbed her, then brushed some more. This time, Storm was denied the luxury of a back-scratching roll. She must remain in the stall where she would stay clean until delivery. For the last time, Lori combed the beautiful blond mane and tail, the features that had attracted her when she first glimpsed the horse from the school bus.

"Shake!" commanded Lori. Storm raised her right foreleg for the ritual both enjoyed. She was glad Storm didn't know why she was crying.

"It's a farewell shake," Lori whispered. Suddenly, she kissed Storm's velvet-soft muzzle.

"It's been nice knowing you," Lori choked. Then, without a backward glance, she closed the barn door and headed for home.

It was already quite dark. If only she could get to the house before her mother walked in the door, she could avert a scolding.

Mike met her at the kitchen door, Mr. Midget peering from beneath his sweater sleeve.

"Hurry!" he said. "Let's get dinner over. Mr. Midget can't wait to open his present. There's one for him hanging on the Christmas tree!"

"And Mike can't wait to open his!"

Lori marveled at the eagerness of a ten-year-old. Once, Christmas had been exciting to her. But not this year. It was almost as though there had been a death in the family.

18

Pioneer Days

VACATIONS WERE USUALLY an anticipated change of pace from the monotony of school. But this vacation was almost a bore. What could Lori do to keep busy and gloss over the void left now that Storm was no longer a part of every day?

Darlene had the major portion of her mural completed. Since the finishing touches on the high parts could be done with the use of a ladder, the scaffolding was no longer necessary. Now Lori and Sandy could paint the murals on either side of the center prize winning one. The janitor and the office force returned to work two days after Christmas so Sandy agreed to go with Lori for several hours each day. They could get more done than they could on school days.

Preoccupation with this project gave Lori a ready-made excuse to avoid Ken. Deep down, she wanted to be with him. But she knew that being around her for long would depress him. Even if she tried to be happy, he wouldn't be fooled. It embarrassed her for him to feel that he must think of ways to cheer her, or to justify his father's actions. Both he and his dad had said that Storm wasn't the only horse, that she could surely find another.

How wrong they both were!

The work on the mural progressed, for the deeper the agony of her loss, the more furiously Lori painted. By the time school was again in session, friends gathered to admire the work that had mushroomed during vacation. Since she was with Sandy so much, she began to appreciate her. The quiet, auburn-haired girl had been an acquaintance. Now Lori regarded her as a friend. She even trusted Sandy with confidential secrets like her feelings about Darlene and how she felt about Ken, something she hoped desperately was mutual. After the long trail rides together, she felt that it was. But she liked hearing Sandy reassure her.

As the days became longer, Lori saw Darlene pass Marycrest more frequently, riding Storm. Although there was a shortcut through the woods to the river from the Silver Spurs Ranch, Lori suspected that Darlene's love for the river trail was heightened by Ken's being there on Rowdy. Of course, the salmon were no longer spawning, but the river area held a fascination for Ken anytime.

Once Lori overheard Randy talking to Mike. Darlene was having trouble controlling Storm. Lori listened hard. Randy said, "Darlene was riding along when suddenly Storm decided to turn onto the power-line trail. She turned real sharp. That made Darlene fall off because she wasn't expecting the horse to do that."

Mike asked, "Was Darlene hurt?"

Randy shook his head. "Her seat was sore for a few days, but she's okay, now."

"Bet she wants Pokey back if she's having trouble with Storm."

"She does. But she's not getting Pokey. Pokey's *my* horse, now."

So Darlene couldn't handle Storm? How interesting! Lori felt smug.

Seeing Darlene on Storm and knowing she was hunting out Ken sent Lori's spirits lower yet. Even her father was beginning to worry about her crushed attitude. He was now back on the job and doing very well, although there was a metal pin at his elbow joint in place of the bone that had once been his elbow. Each day he was getting better use of his arm. He was encouraged.

To try to cheer her up, he offered to go digging for bottles with her. "The dump is still there," he told her. "The arsonist didn't hurt that. Let's go Saturday and see what we can turn up."

The mention of the arsonists reminded Lori that she hadn't heard if the sheriff had found out who they were. She would ask Ken about it next time she saw him.

In answer to her dad's questioning look she said, "Sure. Yes, sure. Let's go digging for bottles. It will be fun." She knew she didn't sound convincing. But she was tired of pretending everything was all right when it wasn't.

Although Lori purposely avoided having to sit by Darlene on the bus, it was a good source of information. Lori had trained herself to pick out Darlene's voice. In this way she learned that Darlene was definitely planning to ride Storm in the Pioneer Days Parade which was scheduled for a part of the Washington's Birthday celebration.

It was a gamble about good weather, but surprisingly, some February days in the past had been warm and sunny. So, according to a report in the weekly local paper, the city fathers had decided to go ahead with plans for an early Pioneer Days Parade.

Darlene on Storm was to be a part of it! According to Darlene, she was going to be an important part. There would be floats depicting pioneer days, with a prize for the best three. There would be prizes for the best costumes among contestants, with costumes for nonriders being judged in another class. Darlene said she had scoured the second-hand stores looking for authentic old clothes. Her aunt had taken her to the city where she had found not only a dress, but high-top laced shoes and an ancient black shawl.

Until now, Lori had thought very little about the Pioneer Days Parade. But Randy and Mike kept teasing her to search out a costume. Lori protested. She didn't have an aunt to take her to every thrift store in a wide radius.

"By the way," said Lori. "When is your aunt leaving?"

Randy's smile faded away. "It's my mom," he said sadly. "Aunt Frieda says we all need her right now. I guess we do. . . ."

"Why?" blurted Mike. "Is your mom sick?"

Randy's eyes searched Mike's face. Was he trying to figure whether or not Mike really didn't know the truth?

"Sort of" was all Randy said.

This brief conversation reminded Lori of her short-lived determination to be a friend to Darlene.

"I meant to do it, too," Lori told herself. "It's

Darlene's fault. Her plot to get Storm spoiled everything!"

She knew that the kind of love she read about in I Corinthians 13 wasn't that fickle. . . . "Love is very patient and kind, never jealous or envious, never boastful or proud, never haughty or selfish or rude. Love does not demand its own way. It is not irritable or touchy. It does not hold grudges and will hardly even notice when others do it wrong. . . ."

She had a marker in her New Testament and she knew these words about love almost by heart. In one way, she longed to know the kind of love expressed here, yet in another way she didn't want to know it at all. There was sort of a fierce satisfaction in being jealous and envious, selfish and rude, irritable and touchy.

Now Lori agreed to the boys' pleadings. She would somehow find a pioneer costume to wear to the parade. It would be better than Darlene's. The little snip would be astride Storm, *her* Storm, long blond hair bobbing rhythmically with the movement of the mare's light tail. But Lori's costume would be better, more authentic. She would go see Mr. Jeffrey that very afternoon. Maybe he had some of his wife's clothes in an old trunk.

Mr. Jeffrey was delighted to see Lori. After greetings and a report on the progress of the mural-painting, she told him the reason for her visit. Mr. Jeffrey's daughter, hearing the conversation, said, "Sure, Pa. Ma's paisley print with the sun bonnet to match is in the trunk in the attic. There are lace-trimmed petticoats, shoes and a shawl. I believe they'd fit Lori, too. Ma was slight and slim like Lori."

The woman left her ironing and returned with the things she had mentioned. When Lori emerged from the bedroom moments later, the old man cried out, "Why, it's our ma come to life! For a fact, it is!"

Lori promised to be careful of the prized antique clothing and Mr. Jeffrey put them in a large grocery bag.

"I'll bring Pa down to the parade," his daughter told Lori. "He'll enjoy it. You might even win a prize."

There was no school on Washington's Birthday. The Pioneer Days celebration dominated the thinking of nearly all the townspeople. The parade and costume judging promised to be the highlight of the day.

Right after lunch, Lori found a place on the curb in front of the Hometown Hardware where she had a good vantage point. Randy had persuaded Mike to ride double on Pokey. Mike knew how his mother felt about horses, but he conveniently neglected to mention his plans to ride. When she looked from the upstairs dentist's office where she worked, as the parade passed, it would be too late for her to forbid his riding bareback with Randy.

Band members were dressed like miners and lumberjacks. Floats depicting pioneer scenes pulled into place behind the musicians, now tuning up. Then costumed riders were assigned positions.

Lori stared as Darlene on Storm came into sight. She fingered the apron of her authentic pioneer costume, confident that she had a good chance of winning a prize. But it didn't matter much. Nothing mattered now that Storm would never be hers.

The crowd gathered quickly, now, and she was glad she had a good place on the curb. Mike and Randy caught her eye and she waved.

Right behind the two boys was Ken on Rowdy! Thinking that Lori was waving at him, he waved back. On impulse, he commanded, "Up, Rowdy, UP!" and the grin flashed in her direction told Lori that Ken was making Rowdy salute her. She blushed and wished her heart would behave. Good old Ken! Dressed like a marshal, complete with badge, he and Rowdy made a handsome pair. Her look of approval must have pushed through to him, because once more Ken commanded, "Up, Rowdy, UP!"

Behind Ken was Sandy and behind Sandy was Darlene.

The band played a number, warming up, then at a signal from the master of ceremonies, struck up a livelier tune, drums pounding, cymbals clashing.

That's when it happened!

Storm went wild! The loud clanging band music set her off, dancing and prancing! She trumpeted loudly, eyes bulging, nostrils distended. She reared and pawed the air, not on command as Rowdy did. It was a desperate attempt to get away from the confusion and noise that jangled her entire being.

Lori gasped. Darlene pulled on the reins, seesawing them and yelling, "Behave, you beast! Storm! Stand still! Stop it!"

"Don't pull the reins like that!" Lori hissed. "You're hurting her mouth. You're making her act wilder!" Now, Lori was coaxing. "Relax, Darlene. Pat her neck. Talk to her. She needs to know you're her friend and everything will be all right . . . oh. . . ."

Lori hardly dared look. Trying to escape the sharp bit that cut her tongue, the horse's huge bulk went back, back. . . . No! She flipped over backwards! That's how hard Darlene pulled on the reins!

Darlene was thrown to the pavement. The

223

reins dangled. Storm, now rid of the pain, realized she was free. She bolted forward, then stopped, hemmed in by the crowd.

Lori knew how confused and bewildered Storm must be. What would the horse do now?

Something had to be done to avert tragedy. But what?

For one split second Lori hesitated, then swung into action!

19

Prizes and Surprises

IN A MOMENT, CAPABLE HANDS were tending to Darlene. Out of the corner of her eye, Lori noted that Dr. Vogan moved forward from the crowd and took charge.

But Storm had to be caught and subdued— and soon. She and Mr. Granberg were possibly the only two who could control the horse. Mr. Granberg was not in sight.

Realizing the potential hazard of a frightened horse loose in a crowd, the man at the loud-speaker warned, "Hold everything, folks. Stand back! Give the young lady a chance. She looks like she's in command. Back! Stand back! That's right. You band players, how about resting?"

Lori approached Storm, calling softly, "Storm, shake! It's me, Lori. You remember me!"

But Storm still pranced, wild-eyed. Knowing the flopping sunbonnet might bother Storm, she slowly pushed it back off her head, then dropped it. She noted that Mike slipped from Pokey to pick up the bonnet. She was glad. She didn't want it dirtied or torn.

"Shake, Storm, shake!"

The horse seemed to listen. Slowly, her ears pricked forward. Up went her right foot. Lori grabbed onto it, shook furiously, then eased her right arm around the horse's neck. Lori relaxed.

Lori smiled at the onlookers. Reaching for the reins with her left hand, she pulled them into position. Then, without thinking whether she was doing the right thing or not, she pulled up her skirt, and swung her right leg over the saddle. Talking quietly to the horse, she held the reins loosely, but firmly. Storm's hind legs wove back and forth, her head bobbed up and down, but she was clearly listening to her rider's commands and obeying in a protesting sort of way.

Controlled applause went up from the crowd. Now the parade master was at Lori's side suggesting that the horse be ridden up a side street and removed from the scene of the parade.

"She'll be all right," Lori assured him. "Let us ride further back from the band. I can handle her, don't worry. How's Darlene? Is she hurt?"

"Just got the wind knocked from her. It's a miracle, I'd say. But she's fine. A bit shaken." Then he smiled. "Her pride's the worst thing hurt."

This was Lori's moment of glory!

Serves Darlene right for snatching Storm away from me! she thought. Suddenly, she hated herself for thinking such a thing. When was she going to start *living* the way she pretended to believe?

"Right now!" Lori said out loud.

She swung the horse around and directed her to the place where Darlene stood on the curb. Lori dismounted.

"Here's your horse," she said, handing the reins to Darlene.

Tears spilled from Darlene's eyes.

"You ride her," she almost yelled. "I never want to get on that horse again! She's possessed. She doesn't do what she's supposed to do. Mr. Bronson can just give me my money back! I'll buy a horse that's been trained by an expert. Not for just a week and then handled by a girl who *thinks* she knows horses — but doesn't!"

Lori bit her tongue to keep from saying what she felt like saying. She stared at Darlene long and hard. Should she take Darlene at her word? Should she mount Storm, ride her in the parade, return her to the Bronson farm as Darlene said? Then she would have a chance to get Storm back! It was the chance she had hoped for, but dared not believe would ever come!

What about that love bit? "Love is very patient and kind, never jealous or envious, never boastful or proud, never haughty or selfish or rude. . . . It does not hold grudges and will hardly even notice when others do it wrong. . . ."

A plan formed in Lori's mind.

She handed the reins to Ken who had come to see if he could help. With deft fingers, Lori loosened Darlene's shiny brown saddle.

"Would you do me a favor, Ken? I know you prefer riding Rowdy bareback, but put Darlene's saddle on Rowdy and use it in the parade, will you?"

Seeing Ken's astonishment, she went on, "We're riding double, Darlene and I. We'd like it better bareback."

Darlene drew back. "You're not getting *me* onto that horse again! Not today. Not ever!"

Lori smiled. "I'll teach you how to handle her another time. She's special. But for today, I'll ride in front, you ride behind." Lori glanced around. "Where's Mike? I need my sunbonnet. Look! Our costumes are quite a bit alike. Those early pioneers never had beautiful saddles like that. They were more likely to ride two at a time, bareback. We might even win a prize, Darlene, the two of us!"

Mike appeared and handed Lori the sunbonnet. She tied it on, after letting Storm see it and explore it with her lips. Bystanders urged Darlene to accept Lori's suggestion. Lori mounted. Ken cupped his hands for Darlene to step into, and she swung into place behind Lori. She clasped her arms tightly around Lori's waist. "Make her mind," she whispered. "Oh, make her mind. . . ."

Lori laughed. "Don't worry, I will."

Suddenly Lori felt lighthearted!

For the first time in many months, Lori's heart knew peace. "Love is never selfish . . . love does not demand its own way . . ." she whispered.

The smile on Lori's face was radiant. Startled from her reverie by the applause of the crowd, Lori's mind returned to the parade. Instinctively,

she handled Storm, just as she had in the months past, and the mare, listening to the familiar voice responded perfectly.

All at once Lori found herself looking straight into a TV camera! She nudged Darlene with her elbow and nodded her head in the camera's direction. Darlene wasn't holding Lori's waist in a viselike grip anymore. She had relaxed and was apparently enjoying being in the parade.

She and Storm will learn to love each other, Lori thought. It's just that Darlene never rode any horse but Pokey and, well, they are different, that's all. It won't take me long to teach her.

"He means us! He means us!" Darlene shouted into Lori's ear. Darlene had been listening to the voice coming over the loudspeaker.

"What do you mean? What did he say?" demanded Lori.

"We're the winners! You were right! Riding bareback won us a prize, first prize!"

The voice invited Lori to bring the horse to the stand so she and Darlene could accept the blue ribbon for the most authentic-looking costumes in the Pioneer Days Celebration.

There, in the front row of spectators, Mr. Jeffrey leaned on his cane, his eyes brimming. "If Carrie only knew," he said. "If Carrie only knew."

Lori accepted the ribbon with a smile. Turning her head, she said to Darlene, "Why don't we give the ribbon to Mr. Jeffrey? This is his wife's dress and it would make him feel good. Okay?"

Darlene gave Lori a happy squeeze of assent and she swung Storm over toward the old man. Lori reached down to hand him the ribbon. Bewildered, he didn't know what to do.

"Take it! Take it!" his daughter said. "Lori wants you to have the ribbon. After all, it was Ma's dress that earned it. Thank you, Lori. Thanks a lot!"

After the parade, there were speeches and refreshments. Storm was given oats and hay at the feedstore parking lot, courtesy of the feedstore, while the girls milled among the crowd, eating hot dogs and munching popcorn.

It was still light when all the festivities were over.

"Let's both ride Storm up the Old Burn Road to your place," Lori told Darlene. "I might as well begin showing you how to handle her."

Darlene agreed and the two set off.

Lori was explaining about how important leg pressure was in riding anything but a kid's horse like Pokey, when Ken caught up to them, riding Rowdy.

"Stop in at Silver Spurs," Ken invited. "Dad has a surprise for you, Lori. He's been shopping.

231

Got two horses in a package deal. You can take your pick or if you don't like either one, he won't make you take one of them. You can find the very horse you want for your trouble of training Storm."

"How about that?" Lori murmured.

Lori never would have believed that she could be interested in owning any horse except Storm. But now that she was letting love rule her thinking and doing, now that she had accepted the fact that Storm was really and truly Darlene's for always, she was anxious to look at another horse. Life without a horse on the Goodman farm was unbearable for Lori and for her father, too, she knew. Mom could be won over, somehow. She would face that when the time came.

Ken pushed the lower gate open, then held it until Storm passed through.

"There's a mare and a gelding," Ken said. "Dad favors the gelding for himself, but you get first choice, Lori."

Making sure the gate was shut all the way, Ken pressed his legs into Rowdy's sides and led the way to the barn. The two girls dismounted while Storm stretched her neck forward nickering loudly. Was she glad to get "home" or was she greeting the two horses she sensed were in the barn?

"Dad and you both lean toward Arabians,"

Ken said. "Of course, these aren't registered. They must be at least half-Arabian, though. They have that look, don't you think?"

At sight of the two horses inside the barn, a little cry escaped Lori's lips. Both were enough to thrill any horse-lover, especially a lover of the sleek look, the arched neck, the dished face with a good width between the eyes.

"They're beauties, aren't they?" Mr. Bronson had come through the barn door. "Think you could go for one of 'em, Lori? Which one meets your fancy? Neither one is Storm, I know. But there are lots of horses in the world besides Storm."

Ken stared hard at Lori. Did he expect her to challenge that statement? Was he wondering how the mask of gaiety had been replaced by the real thing? Did he notice Lori grasp Darlene's hand in genuine understanding and friendship?

No time, now, to clue Ken into the changes in her mind and heart. That could come later.

"Since you favor the gelding, Mr. Bronson, I'll try the mare first," Lori said. Her eyes shone. Taking a bridle from a nail beyond the stall, she talked in quiet tones to the new horse.

"What's her name?"

"Shatze. Little Sweetheart in German."

"Are you and I going to be friends, huh, Shatze?"

233

Ken stood there, holding a saddle. Soon Lori had the mare outside and was ready to mount. She walked Shatze. She galloped Shatze. She gave Shatze her head and let her run around the pasture. Bringing the mare to a stop before the three spectators, Lori laughed a happy, satisfied laugh. "She's great, Mr. Bronson. She behaves beautifully. You're a good shopper!"

Mr. Bronson grinned. "Glad I did better this time," he said. "Looks like everybody is happy and satisfied at last."

He gave Ken a knowing look.

Darlene was the only one not laughing. She stood there watching, listening, unsmiling. What were her thoughts? She did not care to share them evidently, for she said nothing. Then she untied Storm's reins. Only Lori noticed Darlene's indecision. Darlene seemed to want to mount, yet somehow, she did not dare. Was the memory of Storm's wildness too fresh in her mind?

"I can't make myself do it!" Darlene said.

"Sure you can!" urged Lori. "Why don't you tell her to shake? That's how I always did so she'd know the two of us were friends. Then, as you stand up, slip your right arm around her neck and get the reins in place with your left hand. By then, she'll stand still for you to mount. Try it!"

Darlene bit her lower lip and shook her head.

"Ken's dad, here, said it looks as if everybody is happy and satisfied at last. He's wrong. I'm not happy and I'm not satisfied!"

Darlene searched the faces of the three, knowing they were waiting for her to explain what she meant.

Lori, astride Shatze, leaned forward to catch every word.

20

Darlene's Deal

"THE ONLY REASON I WANTED Storm was to spite Lori," Darlene said. "It wasn't that I wanted Storm more than any other horse. Oh, she has class for looks. That's for sure. It was just that I wanted to hurt Lori and that was a way."

Lori listened intently.

"I'd had Storm only a couple of weeks when I wished I had my Pokey back," Darlene went on. "But she was Randy's by then. He and Mike were having so much fun on her, I knew I couldn't ask for her. Let's face it." Darlene looked from one face to another. "I'm not the horsewoman Lori is. I need a safe, steady, dependable horse. Shatze, here, looks more like my type. Mind if I try her, Lori?"

Unable to think of anything appropriate to say, Lori slipped off Shatze and handed the reins to Darlene, taking Storm's reins in exchange.

Speaking quietly to Shatze, Darlene mounted, settling herself in the saddle. She walked the mare around the pasture. Gaining confidence, Darlene urged the horse into a gallop, then into a run. Reining to a halt before the three who had watched her every movement, Darlene's flushed face mirrored the joy that came from a satisfying ride.

"Lori's right! She behaves beautifully! **Lori,** *I* want Shatze!" Darlene paused. "Please?"

"You mean you want me to have Storm?"

Darlene nodded. "Shatze is gentle with just enough spirit." Darlene leaned forward and patted the horse's sleek brown neck. "We can trade. Make it an even trade."

Mr. Bronson, Ken and Lori exchanged looks, astounded.

"But it wouldn't be a fair trade," protested Lori, "would it, Mr. Bronson?"

Ken's dad agreed. "I'm buying three horses with the check that you gave me for Storm, with money left over."

"I have some money I could give you to help even it up," Lori said. "But I don't have *that* much!"

Darlene laughed. "If that's all that's bothering

238

you," she said, "forget it. What do I care about money? Dad banked the money so I could write the check. I'll take Shatze home and put her in the stall and he won't even notice it's another horse. That's how much he cares about what I'm doing."

Darlene pressed her knees into Shatze's sides ever so slightly, clucking at the same time, and took another turn around the field at a gallop.

Reining in, she said, "Is it a deal, Lori? Shatze really is a little sweetheart. Tell me I may keep her, please!"

Lori turned to Mr. Bronson for advice. Having Storm for her very own at Darlene's insistence was surely a switch!

She found it difficult to change gears mentally, after she had finally yielded to the fact that Storm was Darlene's and would never be hers. Darlene's amazing request left her bewildered. Much as she wanted Storm, she didn't want to cheat Darlene.

Mr. Bronson made designs in the damp ground with the toe of his boot.

"Storm's Darlene's horse," he said. "I guess she has the right to trade her if she wants to."

Slowly Lori mounted Storm and, by the way she leaned, told Storm to take a turn around the field. She would have to think this over. Down by the far gate she met Randy and Mike on

239

Pokey, coming home from the parade. Darlene called to the boys to wait.

Returning to where the others still stood, Lori heard Darlene tell Ken, "Take my saddle off Rowdy, if you don't mind. Help me put it on *my* horse, here. Then we'll head for home. I want to show Randy and Mike my new sweetie." She pulled at her dress. "I'm tired of this long skirt. I want to get into jeans and try Shatze on a trail. Okay?"

It was settled, then. Unbelieving, Lori patted Storm and tears of happiness ran down her cheeks.

She thanked Darlene for Storm.

"Don't thank me for letting me have my way," Darlene said. "Now we're all happy and satisfied. Besides, I couldn't go on being mean and spiteful to you, Lori, when you are so nice to me. I mean really nice, not pretend nice."

"We can do a lot of trail riding together," Lori smiled. "I can still teach you some things about horses, maybe. Do you want me to help you teach Shatze to shake hands like Storm does?"

"Great!" Darlene smiled. Ken finished saddling Shatze and Darlene mounted. "Be seeing you!" she called as she rode away.

Lori and Ken looked at each other for a long moment. Then Lori blurted, "Mr. Bronson, mind if I keep Storm here a few days? I can't take her home until just the right moment. I've got a feeling that Dad isn't going to care. But Mom! She's a different story."

Mr. Bronson still shook his head in disbelief. "If Shatze makes her happy, I guess it's all right," he said. "Sure. Put Storm in the first stall. Pick her up when the time comes."

The following day, Lori found a letter in the mailbox as she left the bus. Darlene started home, calling a good-bye as she left, but Lori said, "Wait a second. This letter may interest you." She ripped open the envelope.

Darlene turned back. "Me?"

Lori's eyes scanned the letter. It said the mare known officially as Sada Fari was indeed registered. The certificate had been found among the effects of the man who had given the horse to the boys' school. His heirs, the letter said, had wondered where the mare was so they could deliver the certificate to the new owner.

"Storm is a registered Arabian mare!" Lori told Darlene. "This letter says so. That means she's worth double, probably, what you paid Mr. Bronson for her." Lori paused. Why had she been so curious about papers? But now that she knew, she had to admit it. "Are you sure, Darlene, that you don't want to trade Shatze back so you can keep Storm?"

241

Lori had an anxious moment, wondering what Darlene would say.

Darlene laughed. "What difference does a certificate make, even if it has gold letters on it? Money. But what's money? I'm happy with my Little Sweetheart and I'd be mad at you, Lori Goodman, if you tried to get her away from me!"

Relieved, Lori smiled.

Darlene turned to go, then stopped. "Hey, Lori," she said, "I almost forgot. Aunt Frieda is leaving soon. She wants to see you one more time. It's about those old bottles, I think."

"Sure. When does she want to come over?"

"Maybe right now. I'll dash home, then call you."

An hour later, Darlene and her aunt climbed the steps to Lori's loft. Mrs. Walford fingered the bottles on the loft windowsill.

"My dear," she said, "do you know what you have here?"

"That's an amber corker. I like the shape, don't you? I wonder how they made a bottle look like a log cabin way back in the old days. Dad and I found it a few weeks ago when we went digging."

"It's an Old Homestead Wild Cherry Bitters bottle! Do you have any idea what it's worth?"

"I didn't know it was worth anything. Just thought it was different, that's all."

"It's worth a hundred and fifty dollars, maybe a hundred and seventy-five!"

"Do you mean it?"

"Of course I do. Do you want me to sell it for you?"

"I have another bitters bottle the shape of a fish. It says 1866 on the right side."

"Child! Where did you find all these rare old bottles?"

"Ken found that one the night we explored the old house across from Silver Spurs Ranch."

"Tell you what. I have a flight bag you can fill. Wrap each in tissue so they won't break. I know a man in antiques. I'm almost certain I can send you a check for them in a few weeks."

Mrs. Walford glanced at Lori's clock. "It's been nice knowing you, my dear. So refreshing. I'm glad Darlene shared her friend with me."

Lori smiled. We weren't always friends, she thought. She liked the absence of that heavy feeling she'd had when bitterness and envy crowded her thoughts.

"We'll miss Aunty, won't we?" Darlene said.

"We'll keep in touch." Her aunt smiled.

As Darlene and her aunt left the loft, Darlene paused.

"There's no time for a ride today," she said. "How about tomorrow after school? You promised to help me teach Shatze to shake hands."

"Sure," Lori said. "We can meet at Bronsons'. We'll have a handshaking lesson, then go for a ride in the woods. Maybe Ken can go on Rowdy."

"When are you going to bring Storm here?" Darlene called over her shoulder as she descended.

"I wish I knew," Lori replied. "I wish it was over with. The hassle with Mom about having another horse, I mean." She moved back through the loft door. " 'Bye."

The next afternoon, Ken seemed glad at the offer of company on his daily ride. The two girls used carrots to reward Shatze for her cooperation in the handshaking lesson, and Ken hurried with his chores.

"I'll finish when I get back," Ken said. "Come on. Let's go!"

Every once in a while, Ken left the two girls for a run down the road, then back. Rowdy snorted and puffed, frothing around the bit. Lori felt like scolding Ken for riding Rowdy so hard, but she knew the horse enjoyed the fast spurts as well as Ken did.

While the three walked their horses single file on the trail they were now riding, Ken took a lined paper from his jacket pocket. "Hey," he said, "I almost forgot to tell you. I was snooping around the old cabin across the road and I found a smoldering fire. The house hadn't gone up in flames like whoever set the fire planned."

"They're up to their old tricks!" Lori exclaimed.

"This partly burned paper is notebook paper with the kid's name on it—Kenny Kankelburg. Ever hear of him? He's in trouble, and so are his friends."

"Don't know him," Darlene said.

"There were a couple of papers. I gave the other to the sheriff. Said it was the clue he needed. They suspected who the guys were, but didn't have evidence that would hold water. How do you like that? Your old friend, Ken, has turned detective!"

When they reached the riverbed, the girls walked their horses on the gravel bar while Ken raced Rowdy along the water's edge to a huge boulder, then back.

Lori had been silent as she and Darlene rode side by side. Now, Ken returned and he felt that her mood had changed.

"Anything wrong?" Ken asked Lori.

Lori sighed. "It's just that I'm thinking about Storm—and Mom," she said. "Storm's my horse. Yet I can't take her home for keeps until I have it out with Mom. It's something I dread."

Ken was silent a moment, then said, "It's not going to be any easier by waiting. Why don't you stop by your house on the way back, now?"

Darlene nodded. "Bucky-B's stall is waiting and ready. Why don't you do what Ken says, Lori?"

Lori's knees pressed into Storm's sides, the signal to start up the bank for the ride home.

"I might do that," she said. "I just might!"

21

A Horse for Marycrest

ON THE RETURN TRIP from the river, little was said. Darlene and Ken sensed the struggle going on inside Lori and respected her desire to be alone with her own thoughts.

Tall fir and cedar trees closed in above the narrow little-traveled road, making it seem as though dusk was settling early. Ken led, for Rowdy, as always, insisted on being in the lead. Lori followed Ken, and Darlene came last.

As the trio neared the Goodman property the whir of a chain saw motor filled the air.

"Your dad is working up firewood," Ken called over his shoulder to Lori. "Your mom still work?"

"Yes, but she's probably home by now."

"Could that be her?" Darlene asked. "Looks like she's gardening."

"Yeah," Lori said. "The primroses are out. She's probably weeding. She says it relaxes her."

"Want to turn down this trail to get back to Silver Spurs?" Ken asked. "I don't think your mom's seen us. If we turn now, we'll be hidden by the underbrush. It's your choice, Lori. What do you say?"

Lori hesitated, but only for a moment.

"I might as well get it over with," she said, keeping Storm to the road that passed Marycrest. The other two followed.

"I didn't finish my chores," Ken said. "I'll have to get on back. But I hope you get along OK, Lori. It probably won't be as hard as you think."

Lori forced a smile. Ken was sympathetic with her problem. She appreciated that.

"I'm due home, too," Darlene said. "I've been spending more time with Mother. She's making flowers for her hospital guild. I promised I'd help her when I got back from my ride."

Darlene must have sensed the questions in the minds of the other two. "She's doing OK since Aunt Frieda left. Really great, in fact. Aunty seemed to understand. She knew what to do, too. Things are a lot better at home."

Lori's mother rose from her knees where she

had been weeding a flower bed. She stood watching the three riders. Her jaw suddenly dropped and Lori knew her mother just now realized who the three riders were.

Darlene and Ken both waved a greeting to Lori's mother, before heading on down the road.

"Good-bye," Lori told Ken. "Wish me luck!"

"You'll do all right," he said, and he was gone.

This was it!

Lori walked Storm up the Marycrest circular driveway and reined the horse in beside her mother.

Lori dismounted, reins in hand. She and her mother looked at each other a moment before either one spoke.

"She's mine, Mom," Lori said softly. "Storm's my horse. Mine to keep."

"What do you mean?" She sensed a quiver in her mother's voice.

While Lori wondered how to begin, her mother asked, "Isn't this the horse that's been in Bronsons' pasture?" She removed her gardening gloves slowly, deliberately. "Seems like I heard — I don't remember where — that Darlene bought her for a fabulous price. Wasn't that Darlene you were with just now? What horse was she riding?"

Suddenly, it became easy to spill out the entire story.

Mrs. Goodman pulled her gloves on and stooped to weed again while her daughter talked. Lori could see that her mother was struggling with her emotions.

"Please understand, Mom," Lori pleaded. "I knew you'd never be able to let yourself say 'yes' if I asked if I could have another horse — especially Storm, with the reputation she had when she first came to Bronsons'."

Lori studied her mother's face, wanting to hear her reaction, yet dreading to hear it, too.

"It was being sneaky, it's true," Lori went on, "going off to Silver Spurs for my daily session with Storm. I shouldn't have, I guess. But I did. Anyway, that part's history, now. The exciting thing is that I own a horse, a beauty of a horse. And she's been trained by an expert, Mom. Mr. Granberg put a lot of hours on her. You don't have to be afraid, Mom, really!"

Lori's mother slipped to a sitting position on the walk beside the flower bed. She bit her lip.

"Yes, it was wrong of you to be deceptive, Lori, I agree." She brushed a wisp of hair from her face with the back of her hand. "But perhaps I drove you to it. As I heard your dad say, an accident, even a serious accident, shouldn't mean there can't ever be a horse in any of our lives again. Not when you and your dad love them so. . . ."

Lori breathed easier. She leaned against Storm, savoring the softness of Storm's muzzle against her own cheek. Now Storm explored Lori's hair with her lips.

"You tickle!" Lori told Storm, then turned back to her mother. "Oh, Mom! You're not mad? It's all right if Storm is mine? Can I put her in Bucky-B's stall . . . now?"

"I guess I know when I'm licked."

The chain saw was silent. Mother and daughter were unaware that Mr. Goodman was approaching, but suddenly, there he stood.

"Licked?" he echoed. "It's not often I hear you say that, Katherine. What's going on?" He didn't wait for an answer. "Hadn't you better be getting Bronsons' horse back to him, Lori? I assume he loaned her to you so you and Ken could go riding."

Lori grinned. "Storm's mine."

"You're teasing!"

"No, I'm not, Dad. Storm really is mine!" Lori explained to her dad how it had come about.

A smile crept over Lori's dad's face, a smile that wouldn't wipe off. He patted Storm's muzzle. He stood back and eyed her. He picked up one hoof, then another, for inspection.

"I can't believe it. I just can't believe it!"

"She's a registered Arabian, Dad. I have the papers."

"You don't say! I'd never dared to hope such an animal would come to live at Marycrest." He stroked the horse's sleek side. "And to think you managed the transaction without a penny coming from any of our pockets!"

"See what I mean?" Lori's mom said. "I guess I know when I'm licked. The two horse-lovers in the family win out against the fearful mother. Actually, I love watching a horse in motion. I'm glad when one will let me stroke it. But if I try to imagine myself up on its back, I shiver all over!"

Lori laughed. "We'll have you riding Storm, too, Mom. I'll give you pointers. Want to try?"

"I'll get my thrills by watching you ride, Lori."

Mike came out the front door and bounded down the steps.

"What's happening?" he demanded. "What's Storm doing over here, Lori?"

"I've brought her home — for keeps!"

"You mean it? Hey, that's great!" Mike looked first at Mom, then at Dad to see if Lori was telling the truth.

"You don't have to be afraid, Mom," Mike said. "It was great the way Lori quieted Storm when she acted up in that parade. You should have seen her. She was real brave the way she. . . ."

"I did see her," Mom said. "I just happened to look out the office window and I saw every bit.

Only I didn't know it was Lori. Others told me, later. I wasn't that close and I wasn't used to seeing her in that long dress." She gathered up her gardening tools. "Lori, are you sure that horse is safe? She sure looked out of hand to me!"

Lori's dad spoke up. "Lori brought her under control like a pro, I'm told. That's to her credit."

Mrs. Goodman sighed. "You're right, I suppose, Edward. I heard the same thing from several people who came into the office. It wasn't the fact that Lori won a prize for her costume that impressed anyone. It was the way she handled that horse! It got me to thinking. 'I haven't been fair with my daughter,' I've been telling myself. And now you own that horse! Actually, I should give my fears to the Lord. I know that. I'm working on it."

The glance Lori's dad gave her mother said, "Good for you, Katherine."

A sudden impulse overwhelmed Lori. Handing the reins to her father, Lori threw her arms around her mother and squeezed her.

Mr. Goodman grinned and Mike blurted, "Mom, you're pretty when you're happy."

"I'm glad Storm is yours, Lori," she said. "Really glad. Believe me."

Lori turned to face Storm.

"Shake!" she commanded the horse.

Storm raised her right front hoof. Lori grasped it, pumped it up and down. "Howdy, Storm, old girl," Lori said. "Welcome to Marycrest Farm!"

"Would you look at that, Katherine," Lori's dad breathed. "Lori, will she shake hands with me?"

Lori moved over. "Try it."

Her dad gave the command and Storm responded.

"Stand right by me, Edward. Let me try shaking hands with Storm."

Mom was won over! Lori glowed.

She wouldn't be satisfied, though, until her dad had discovered the joy of riding Storm. How that would be brought about, she didn't know. But it just had to happen!

Lori's heart sang.

Once again, at Marycrest, there would be the sound of pounding hooves!